Henry and Anthony

To order additional copies, please contact us.
BookSurge
www.booksurge.com
1-866-308-6235
orders@booksurge.com

Henry and Anthony

H. Lynn Beck

2009

Dedication

I thank my three children: Kevin, Nicholas and Christi-anne, my beautiful daughter. They are, and will always remain, my greatest accomplishment, my dearest friends, and my heros.

I am forever grateful for my best friend, Dona Katia.

To my students at Southern Illinois University at Edwards-ville, who have laughed at my jokes, listened to my goose stories, and encouraged me to write this book, I am grate-ful.

And to my grandfather Tyler, who always loved geese and to my Uncle Wayne and Aunt Lucille, who were just sim-ply, and unconditionally, my friends

Prologue

This is an unlikely, and perhaps, unbelievable story; yet, it is true. All facts have been related to me by someone who either witnessed the events or participated in them. Why they selected me to write their story is a mystery. In spite of my warnings that I was not a writer, they insisted on telling me their story, and that I put it into our words and tell it to others. I believe the story must be told, even if my words are not the most eloquent. It is a simple story that began only a few years ago on the campus of a small university in southern Illinois—Southern Illinois University at Edwardsville (SIUE).

chapter

ONE

Mother Goose, and her partner, Father Goose, have been together for years and have successfully produced many batches of fine goslings. In all this time Father Goose has never lost an egg or a gosling to a predator. He is very proud of this achievement. But Mother Goose is worried.

This spring, for reasons unknown to Mother Goose, she produced only one egg. In the many years that she and Father Goose had been together, she always produced many eggs, each one resulting in a beautiful gosling. She did not understand how she could only produce one egg. She worried that it might not hatch, or if her only gosling died, she would have no other. Her heart was sad. She could not imagine a year without the daily joy of raising her goslings. Each day she worried more and more; and, to compensate, she became increasingly dedicated to caring for her only egg. She was hesitant to leave it, even to go to the pond to drink or to swim to relax, or even to eat.

At night, sometimes Father Goose watched the sadness in Mother Goose's eyes as she sat on their egg. Father Goose recognized her determination as she seemed to will life into the egg. Father Goose wanted to comfort her, so he left his position of guarding the nest and began honking softly to her as he approached Mother Goose. Father Goose said nice things to encourage her. He reminded her that the number of eggs, or the number of goslings, did not matter. One gosling, or a dozen, they were each special and blessed by the Great Goose. He used his beak to caress the neck of Mother Goose to make her feel warm and special. Mother Goose tried to smile, but the depth of her sadness made it difficult. Father Goose told her that the Great Goose had a special reason for sending them only one egg this year. Even though she, Mother Goose, had laid the egg; it was the Great Goose that created the egg and sent it to her. Perhaps the solitary egg was to have a special destiny. Father Goose had spent many hours thinking about why, this year, after so many other years, the Great Goose had limited their nest to only one egg. The only conclusion that could be made was that their egg was special and their gosling would also be special. Father Goose was certain that they needed to focus all their abilities on that one egg and, after it hatched, on the solitary gosling. Father Goose reminded Mother Goose that they had always unconditionally loved whatever the Great Goose had sent. He reminded her that they should not now doubt His wisdom.

As the days passed, Mother Goose shed her sadness and began to accept Father Goose's point of view. She renewed her daily visits to the pond, and Father Goose thought he saw more energy in her walk. She no longer viewed their one egg as a personal failure. She again had purpose in her life.

A few days after Mother Goose started sitting on her egg, a dog approached as dusk descended upon the nesting area. It had a collar, so it was not a wild dog. Father Goose knew by its movements that it was not a dog accustomed to fighting for food. Its actions were not purposeful, but like a dog out for a walk without the confinement of a leash. Both Mother Goose and Father Goose watched its every move as it came over the hill. Mother Goose shifted her wings to ensure that her egg was safely under her and lowered her head so that she was difficult to be seen and made ready to attack, if necessary. She watched the dog's every movement. Father Goose stood silently from his guarding position, spread his wings to their full length and slowly relaxed them; he stretched his neck until it was fully extended and positioned his head close to the ground. Father Goose was also in attack position.

The dog went from here to there, sniffing the ground, then a bush, and then the ground again. He stopped and sniffed and then ran a few steps and sniffed again. When he came inside Mother Goose and Father Goose's territory, Father Goose advanced a few steps and hissed. The dog stopped and his eyes squinted as he focused in the direction of the hiss. Father Goose took a few steps. The dog cocked its head first to the left, then to the right, then held it high, and sniffed repeatedly, unable to identify the smell.

The dog continued a few paces and stopped again. Father Goose also advanced a few steps, puffed out his chest, and repeated his hissing warning. The dog took one more step and stopped. He had never seen a goose so close before. Although he was not well acquainted with the dangers of the outdoor world, he was curious. When the dog shifted its weight to take its next step, Father Goose decided that his family was in danger. He launched himself towards the dog, hissing and honking with all his speed and fury. The dog's eyes opened wide. He had not expected the goose to charge him, and he looked so much larger now. When Father Goose extended his wings his chest tripled in width. The dog decided that the best action was to retreat, which he did, speedily.

The danger over, Father Goose strutted past Mother Goose, chest fully expanded, as he proudly returned to his guarding position. As he passed near Mother Goose, he turned his head toward her and smiled. He was very proud of his ability to defend his family.

After 28 days, Mother Goose's gosling was stirring inside the egg and started to break the shell from the inside with his beak. An anxious Mother Goose helped him break the shell from the outside. The gosling raised its head and looked around.

Father Goose, sensing the occasion, came as quickly as a goose can on land. He smiled at Mother Goose. He rubbed her neck with his beak and honked repeatedly in a low tone. They decided to name their special gift from the Great Goose, Henry.

During the night, Henry practiced his standing and walking ability before he fell asleep safely under Mother Goose's warm plumage. The next morning Mother Goose proudly led him to the pond. He followed in spurts and stops and bursts that led to spills. He attempted to see everything: the grass, the pond, the sky, and the other goslings. Each time he spied something interesting, he tripped over a stick or a clump of grass. Several times Mother Goose stopped and waited for Henry to catch up with her. She proudly squawked softly for Henry to refocus on following her. Father Goose brought up the rear as a hind guard. As he walked, he looked to the left and then to the right. Sometimes he stopped and stared into a clump of bushes before deciding it was safe to continue after his family.

Mother Goose approached the pond, and without slowing or hesitating, walked straight into the water and started swimming. Henry, placing all his trust in his mother, followed. He stopped promptly when he felt the temperature and texture of water. It was a new, yet a wonderful feeling. He briskly vaulted into the pond as only a young creature can do. To his surprise, Henry found that he too could swim. In fact, he discovered that he was much better at swimming than he was at walking. There were no sticks or clumps of grass to impede his progress. Father Goose reached the water's edge; he was proud of his son's boldness. After a quick pause, and a careful look around, Father Goose followed the others into the water.

Henry was not the only gosling to break through his shell that spring. Shells all over the university campus cracked open within days of each other with many goslings making their first appearance into a strange world. Everywhere mother geese were examining their goslings as fathers welcomed them. When the sun appeared, the mothers formed their goslings into a line and marched them to the water. The fathers followed at a distance to protect their families.

The arrival of the goslings created a new distraction for people at the university: watching the new families walk to and from the pond, and swimming on the pond. The parent geese were very gentle, patient, and watchful over their offspring, but also very defensive. The father geese challenged any person or animal that did not maintain a safe distance between them and the goslings, even other geese are not allowed close to their goslings. And one does not negotiate with a goose protecting its family. When a goose hisses at you, you should retreat. The alternative is to experience the horror of a 15-pound bowling ball flying towards you with flapping wings spread across six feet of air with an opened beak screaming insults.

Parent geese allow the goslings to wonder about to explore their surroundings, but they always maintain themselves near the goslings and are always vigilant for anything that comes too close. Even if the goslings approach other geese, the parent geese put their heads down, hiss, and attack until the non-family geese back away enough to satisfy the parent geese. Sometimes, the parent goose pursues a group of geese two or three times until they are confident that enough distance is put between their goslings and the other geese.

The other geese always comply with the parent geese's wishes without any fighting. All geese seem to understand the parent geese's need to protect their young. It is as though each day is revealed as a play written by geese where all geese are born knowing exactly how to act all parts, and each does so without missing a beat. Harmony always exists in a geese gaggle.

The campus is a peaceful place, with the exception of an occasional hostile encounter between man and goose, but danger still exists for geese. Some animals would be delighted to eat a careless goose, and many more would enjoy a gosling, if the opportunity presented itself. So, Henry had to develop many skills to stay alive and safe. He quickly learned to swim and walk. He learned to distinguish sounds and expertly detect any sudden movement that may imply danger. He learned to obey Mother and Father Goose without any hesitation. Goslings that fail to learn this lesson die very young. The goose world does not forgive slow learners.

Henry was happy and certain he had learned all he needed to know. He desperately wanted to explore. Sometimes he darted away from his mother and father to investigate a butterfly, a rabbit, or a strange sound, but then his mother or father immediately honked their disapproval, and he grudgingly returned. To Henry, the world was so big and strange and exciting. His ability to maneuver on land improved each day as did his ability to recognize most animals' sounds and determine which were dangerous.

When Henry was two weeks old, a household cat was on the prowl at night, and it spotted the nest with Henry and Mother Goose. Cats, like dogs, are not very familiar with geese, but this cat viewed Henry as a good meal. The cat advanced slowly, crouching close to the ground. He flattened his ears and kept his head down to maintain a stealthy profile. He focused on Mother Goose. The cat had convinced itself that if he hissed and attacked quickly and suddenly; she would flee the nest leaving the gosling unprotected. Unfortunately, this cat was not familiar with geese's loyalty to its family.

The cat did not see Father Goose and was not aware that every step was being watched by both Mother and Father Goose. As the cat crossed an invisible line where Mother and Father Goose upgraded their view of the cat from a possible danger to an imminent threat, Father Goose advanced, hissing and honking with wings and head outstretched, and his head lowered close to the ground. For geese, this was a clear and final message, "If you come one step closer, I will attack you." The cat had never seen, nor heard, anything like this, and it did not want to meet anything like this again. It quickly disappeared.

Henry did not wake because Mother Goose felt sufficiently safe that she did not move. She had watched everything, but the threat was never sufficient for her to transmit fear to Henry. She had every confidence in Father Goose. Father Goose hurried back to Mother Goose and when he was approaching, he slowed is pace, raised his head and walked deliberately to show Mother Goose that he was in good health and fine form and that she and Henry would always be safe with him on guard. Mother

Goose smiled at him. Father Goose did not turn to look at her, but he saw her smile and his heart pumped faster.

The next day while Henry was swimming, he noticed a family of goslings nearby. He wanted to play with them, so, suddenly he turned toward them. Henry wanted to make friends; however, this was not allowed by the parent geese until the goslings were properly prepared and old enough. Parent geese teach their goslings the necessary survival skills before allowing them to socialize. For defensive reasons, the parent geese often stay near other parent geese and maintain the same daily schedules. When one pair of geese takes their goslings for a swim, several pairs of geese accompany them; however, the parent geese do not interact with the others, and never do the goslings leave their parents' sides. They form convoys for safety. If a hungry coyote was in the area and saw the geese, he would never find a safe opportunity to snatch a goose or a gosling. With several pairs of geese in the same area, the coyote would be detected and chased away by several fathers while the mothers protected the young as one group. Consequently, when Henry attempted to make friends, his parents, or the parents of the other gosling, quickly honked a warning. Henry always returned, but he very much wanted to play with the other goslings.

Each night, when Mother Goose and Father Goose sat with Henry, before Henry slept and before Father Goose took guard duty, Henry asked questions. Henry was a very keen gosling and wanted to know everything. He asked, "Where did I come from?"

Mother Goose and Father Goose looked knowingly at each other. Mother Goose replied, "Why, Henry, you came from inside the egg. Have you forgotten already? Do you remember when I helped you out?"

Henry thought a little, and then asked, "But mama, who put me in the egg?"

Mother Goose smiled and she answered, "The Great Goose gives us all life Henry. He is the one that makes us and guides us."

"Does He guide you, Mama?"

"Of course, he does Henry. He guides everyone."

"How does He guide you, Mama? Why can't you find your own way?"

"He talks to us, Henry. He is the one that invited us to live on this pond. He is the one who warns us when danger approaches and helps us when we have problems we must solve."

Again, silence from Henry, but Mother and Father Goose saw the wheels turning in Henry's head. "Mama, what does the Great Goose's voice sound like?"

Mother Goose again smiled. "Henry, the Great Goose does not speak like you or me. He speaks through our minds. He places a thought or an action in our mind. We must be wise enough to understand that He is guiding us and to follow his wishes."

"Mama, does the Great Goose speak to all the geese, or just you?"

"Henry, He speaks to all geese, but not every goose hears Him speak. Some geese have not been trained to hear His voice, or to believe in Him enough to do what He is telling them to do."

"Mama, how do we know when it is the Great Goose who is speaking and not someone else? How do we know if we are only talking to ourselves or some other goose is talking to us?"

"Henry, this requires some experience, but the Great Goose will not ask you to do something that is bad," said Mother Goose. "With time, you learn to separate your thoughts from the messages sent by the Great Goose and you will learn to trust Him."

"Mama, how did the Great Goose fit me into the shell without breaking it?"

"Oh, Henry, you ask so many questions. You must be patient. Life will answer many questions for you, but there is one thing that you must always remember, Henry. Not all geese can hear the Great Goose's voice. Some geese are deaf to His advice. These geese can hear nothing that He says. Some geese even say that He does not exist. You must become a goose that can hear the Great Goose's words and never doubt them."

"Mama, what do I have to do to be able to hear His words?"

"You must train your mind, Henry. You must keep the Great Goose in your heart and in your mind while always maintaining pure thoughts. You must never think bad things or say bad things. You must always believe in what is good and, if you do, good things will always happen. If you do this each day of your life, you will be able to hear the Great Goose's words, and accept guidance from Him. He will help you, and He will help you to help others. A strong goose must always help a weaker goose."

Henry fell silent for a moment. Mother and Father Goose looked at each other and smiled. Then Henry asked, "What if the Great Goose asks me to help someone, but when I help them, someone else is hurt?"

Mother Goose took a moment to formulate her thoughts. She said, "Henry, I cannot speak for the Great Goose. I can only tell you what I think His intentions are. I think that one example would be two geese fighting. We can assume you have two alternatives. You could help the first goose win the fight with the second goose. When the first goose wins the fight, he kills the second goose. Your second alternative could be to help the second goose win the fight with the first goose. When this fight is won, the second goose walks away and allows the first goose to walk away also. In the first situation, you helped to kill a goose. In the second situation, you helped to save the life of a goose. The Great Goose does not favor killing. It is horrible to think about this. I can only imagine He might ask you to kill if it saves more lives, but do not think these thoughts now. You must sleep."

Mother Goose became emotional. These discussions occurred every night, and Henry demonstrated that he was a very thoughtful and intelligent goose, much beyond the typical goslings. He revealed thoughts that many adult geese did not have their entire life. She thought this might be the right moment to tell Henry of other thoughts that she and Father Goose had. She said, "Henry, your father and I think you are very special. We believe you have been blessed with the ability to hear the Great Goose's messages. We believe completely in the Great Goose and the necessity of listening carefully for his guidance, and following it. We do not know if we hear all His messages. We only know that we hear many of them."

Mother Goose paused, looked at Father Goose, and continued, "We believe He has told us that you are special in His eyes. We believe He has some special use for you. We do not know what it is, but we want you to be prepared for it. We want you to have your mind trained so that you can recognize the Great Goose's voice when He speaks. You must be able to distinguish it from thrill-seeking ideas or common ideas that young geese often have. We believe you have been given special talents, which you will be asked to share for the happiness of others. We do not know what these talents are, but Henry, we must work with you each day to train your mind so you will be ready."

Henry listened and replied, "Yes, Mama. Mama, I'm tired. I think I'll sleep now. Goodnight Mama. Goodnight Papa." Henry disappeared under Mother Goose's wing and almost immediately, Henry was asleep.

Mother Goose and Father Goose looked at each other and wondered if Henry would be ready. They knew they must continue to teach him, but they had to trust in the Great Goose. Mother Goose sat close to Henry and extended her wing over him. She felt Henry lean his head on her feathers. Father Goose distanced himself to assume his guard position.

Within 10 weeks, Henry had learned to fly. He still had to become strong enough to fly long distances over many hours and keep pace with the gaggle. Each day, Henry gorged himself and grew rapidly. As he increased in size and weight, grew feathers, and improved his muscle condition, his coordination improved and he flew better. The gaggle did not wait for a slow flier. If he fell behind, he would become an easy target for a predator.

One night, when Mother Goose and Henry were asleep, Father Goose grew tense. He instinctively knew danger was approaching. At first, he thought that the dog or cat had returned, and then he realized that it was not a dog; it was a coyote. Coyotes were worse than dogs. They hunted to eat. Dogs did not hunt. They only sniffed around. Dogs had no specific objective. Then he saw that there were two coyotes, probably a couple. The coyotes split and approached slowly from two directions. They were not afraid of Father Goose. He made a sound to wake Mother Goose. She woke Henry and told him not to move or make a sound. He understood and obeyed.

Father Goose watched the larger of the two coyotes, probably the male, while Mother Goose watched the smaller of the two. These coyotes were not easily deterred. Father Goose took a few steps, spread his wings and with his head low, he hissed loudly. The coyotes stopped, but after a couple seconds, they continued a zigzag course towards the nest. Both geese knew a fight was inevitable and that their survival was not guaranteed. These coyotes were not afraid. Mother and Father Goose would have to win, or they would all die.

Father Goose did not allow the coyote to advance. Since the coyote would not frighten, it would be foolish to allow him to approach closer. Father Goose charged him. He gained speed, half running and half flying. He held his wings out and hissed and honked and grabbed the coyote, who also grabbed Father Goose. A great ruckus was heard for a long distance in the quiet evening on the college campus. It was obvious to all that heard it that it was a life and death struggle. The sounds from both Father Goose and the coyote made it clear that the struggle was serious.

Father Goose and the coyote were going in circles, but Father Goose knowingly moved the struggle away from the nest. Father Goose felt bites in many places, but he was aggressive and never allowed the coyote to sustain a hold on him. Father Goose broke each coyote's bite and grabbed something else, and the coyote howled again, and then the coyote broke Father Goose's hold, and the cycle repeated many times. On and on it went, with no one carrying a clear advantage over the other.

Meanwhile, Mother Goose had her eyes glued on the other coyote. She knew that the other coyote would use the distraction of the fight to attack. She was ready. When the female coyote started her run toward the nest, Mother Goose advanced to meet her. She would never allow the female coyote close to her Henry. She hissed and squawked and honked, also half flying and half running. They met, and the ensuing noise was added to those already filling the night. It was impossible to know who was winning. Henry only heard noises confirming that both his Mama and Papa and the coyotes were giving and receiving bites. Henry was very afraid. He understood that all their lives were in jeopardy; yet, he knew that his Mama and Papa would win. No one could defeat his Mama and Papa.

The female coyote broke off the fight first. She yelped with futileness and left the scene without delay. The male coyote knew that without a coordinated attack, winning was hopeless, and tried to make a graceful retreat. But Father Goose was not in a forgiving mood. He chased the coyote and made one last bite. When he felt the coyote's soft tissue in his beak, he crunched it with all his might. He stopped running and braced his feet. The coyote tried to run, but it was difficult to drag an angry, 15-pound goose with its stiffened legs extended as brakes. The coyote was pulling Father Goose uphill as he moved away from the pond, all the while howling in pain.

When Father Goose was satisfied there was no more danger, he released the coyote, whose retreat could be traced by the pitiful cries. Father Goose returned quickly to the nesting area. He saw that Henry was untouched and that Mother Goose was alive and honking softly to Henry. Both Father and Mother Goose suffered cuts and bruises and were very sore for several days. They each rubbed their beaks against the other's body and thanked the Great Goose for their survival.

Father Goose was proud he had never lost a fight. Any animal defeated in battle usually died. It was important that Mother Goose and Henry have confidence in him as their protector. And they did. They had total confidence that they were safe with him by their side. He was sore but extremely proud. He returned to his guard position and sat. He must not sleep because it was early and other predators might attempt to take advantage of their cuts and sores and tiredness. All the valley's animals knew of the struggle.

By mid-July, Henry was flying. He practiced every day and quickly became stronger as he flew longer and longer distances. For Henry, it was easy. All the goslings were doing it, but Henry felt he was the best. He was certain that no gosling could fly as well as him. Henry flew at every chance. He flew over things, under things, around things. This worried his mother and father, because flying was not a sport. It was what you did to live, to survive. You had to be strong, consistent, and group-oriented. Goose life did not have room for play, especially individual play.

Geese survive by being vigilant of the group. When they fly in the V-formation, the lead goose has to work much harder than the other geese. Those that follow gain lift from the lead goose's work. This energy conservation is achieved by all other geese flying in this formation; and for this, they honk encouragement to their leader.

When a leader tires, a new leader replaces him. This allows geese to fly up to 18 hours a day, covering 750 miles, depending on wind speed. They do not depend on a single leader. Leadership is a revolving responsibility. All geese are able to lead and to follow. They know when to assume leadership and when to relinquish it. This keeps the gaggle strong.

When a goose becomes sick or wounded, and cannot keep pace while flying in the gaggle, one or two other geese follow him to land, and protect him. If the goose improves, they continue their journey and rejoin their gaggle. If the goose dies, the others return to the gaggle as best as they can.

Henry understood the need for families and gaggles to stay together and work together, but he loved to do things that other geese did not do. He liked flying alone just above the grass line. He loved to feel the grass touch his wings as he sped across the hills following the contour of the land. When the land and grass dipped, so did he. When the land and grass surged, so did he. He loved to fly to higher altitudes and throw himself at the ground by tucking his wings and allowing gravity to have its way with him. He learned when he had to extend his wings to defeat gravity, and how to lean to deny gravity its wish of burying him in the dirt.

Soon, flying close to the ground did not excite Henry, so he invented new games. He entered wooded areas. He jumped into the air and hugged the grass as he flew straight toward a tree. At the last possible second, he maneuvered his wings to rotate himself 90 degrees on his horizontal axis and flew around the tree. Then, he returned to a horizontal position and lined up another tree. He flew straight towards it and around the other side, rotating 90 degrees on his horizontal axis in the opposite direction.

Henry always practiced flying fast, close to the ground, and around trees. He grew stronger and gained better timing and coordination. He found areas where the trees were spaced closer, and he practiced until he could fly around them from both directions. He learned how to judge his speed and the distance of the trees to better adjust his movements. He could look ahead at two or three trees and know his next two or three moves. Henry loved flying as much as he loved to eat.

chapter

TWO

Fall came and then winter and still Henry continued to practice his flying skills. After the leaves dropped from the trees, he practiced flying around the trees near the campus buildings. He now had a clear view of the trees, the people, and the buildings. The trees were closer together in this area, and he did not yet have the flying skill to fly around each tree, so he flew around two each time. As he practiced, he became more skilled. Soon, Henry could dart quickly around each tree. Henry turned corners that were so sharply angled that when he rotated to change direction, he flew sideways. His wings felt great stress, but this only increased the strength of his bones and his confidence.

Henry always practiced flying alone. The other geese showed no interest in joining him. Henry did not understand why they did not enjoy flying like he did. Each time he completed a difficult move, he felt a wonderful sensation inside his mind. It was satisfying. Each success pushed him to complete more difficult maneuvers. He never tired. He always wanted more.

When the trees offered little challenge, Henry went to the university's entrance. It had light poles located along a curving road just below the crest of a hill. Scattered among these poles were informational signs. After the sign that announced the location of the tennis courts, the road ended abruptly. Drivers turned right or left. The tennis courts were located on the other side of the road and had high fences with green strips woven among the wires. The green strips caused the tennis courts to blend seamlessly into the surrounding green grass.

At this intersection, Henry turned left and then swung further to his left to miss a light pole. Then, to avoid the transparent bus stop, he increased his altitude by a few feet. Usually, there were students sitting inside this area waiting for a bus. Mostly, they did not see him, but only sensed the passage of his shadow.

Beyond this bus stop were two light poles which Henry passed to the right and then to the left before he turned sharply to the right and flew over the parking lot, through the trees, and over a large classroom building. Henry liked this course and practiced flying it from both directions.

Rumors spread among the geese about Henry's unnatural obsession with flying. Geese fly as other animals walk, because they must. In the animal world, dogs did not practice lifting their legs; cows did not practice chewing their cud, and geese did not practice flying. Mother and Father Goose had discussed the possibility that Henry's obsession with flying might be the Great Goose's special gift. Many of the geese in the gaggle honked about crazy Henry, but when Mother or Father Goose appeared, they stopped. Mother and Father Goose knew that the other geese had been gossiping about Henry. They were dismayed at such needless honking, because not all goslings were alike and should not be expected to be the same. Occasionally, one gosling, or another, was given a very special talent by the Great Goose. The gaggle benefited from these special talents. They were upset that Henry was being discussed in such negative ways because of his special talent. They would not tolerate it and always scolded the geese who did it, but it continued anyway.

Whatever Henry's destiny, it was the Great Goose's gift to Henry. Mother and Father Goose wanted for Henry to be sufficiently strong to discover it, to defend it, to perfect it, and to follow it. That is what a strong goose must do, so Mother and Father Goose ensured Henry was strong. They still believed that Henry, last year's only egg, was special.

Eventually, spring arrived. Henry had grown into a fine young goose. He still loved to play. He continued to practice his flying, but he paid more attention to his environment. When he lined up with the other geese to eat grass, he tried to casually wander towards a nice young gander that he liked. These attempts were always stopped within seconds when Henry's mother, or the mother of the young gander, became aware of Henry's intention and would maneuver him back into position and away from the innocent gander.

Henry preferred an area where short cut grass surrounded a patch of taller, uncut grass. The short grass was mowed to keep it neat and beautiful. The taller grass was allowed to grow without interference from machines. The objective was to allow the tall grass to mature naturally and produce seed, and reseed itself. Eventually, the university wanted the grassy area to return to its natural composition when man first found it growing.

When the gaggle reached this island of tall grass, half of the geese went on one side and the other half went on the other. Henry had difficulty concentrating on eating. When he raised his head, he could see the geese on the other side. From the other side, a young gander raised her head and saw Henry. Henry was startled and dropped his head quickly. Then, curiously, he raised it to see if the gander was looking. She was, but she was also startled and dropped her head to hide behind the grass.

Soon, this was a game. Henry looked, and as soon as the gander peaked, he would quickly drop his head. Then, after a few seconds, Henry would raise his head, and the gander would drop her head. Very quickly, other young geese understood the game, and they joined. When Henry's mother looked around for Henry, she saw several young geese on each side of the tall grass raising and lowering their heads in synchronized fashion. She honked disapprovingly, and all the young geese quickly returned to the continually advancing eating line.

Occasionally, some of the other young geese teased Henry about his stunt flying. They equated it with the inability to fly properly. This should surprise no one because when the geese elders spoke deridingly of Henry's past-time, the younger geese listened and copied their behavior and soon also made fun of him. They questioned and probed Henry about his ability to fly. They did not believe Henry could fly better than other geese. Henry listened graciously to it for a few weeks, but one day he had had enough.

Henry was not mean-spirited, but he was intelligent. He felt this teasing would not stop until he stopped it. So one day when he heard a group of young geese making fun of him, Henry bravely approached. They fell silent and watched him as he approached the young goose that Henry thought was the leader. He told the young geese to pick their four best fliers. The four and Henry would play "Follow the Leader." It would be a two-part test. First, Henry would be leader and could select any course he wished to fly. The other four geese would have to follow very closely on his wing. Any goose that could not keep up would lose the competition and go home defeated. Second, the four geese would select a leader, who could fly any course he wished. Henry would have to follow on the other team leader's wing and keep pace, or he would lose. They agreed, thinking that it would be fun and easy.

To warm up, Henry took them towards the university's entrance and was already increasing his altitude. He made a wide loop toward the northeast, always increasing his altitude. He was taking them much above the altitude geese normally use for flying. The team of four geese had never flown at that altitude before and they honked mockingly and laughed at Henry. They accused him of being afraid to start the course. Unfortunately for them, they had never witnessed Henry at play before. Henry said nothing. He continued to maneuver into the perfect position. Once he was high and on the north side, he turned towards the south and lined up on the university's entrance road. When Henry was ready, he honked to the other geese to inform them that the course was officially starting. He folded his wings and dropped his long neck toward Earth. Gravity pulled Henry swiftly toward the university entrance. The other geese were caught off guard. They had never seen this before and were not expecting this action. Henry approached Earth at lightening speed, while the other geese descended as they normally did—slowly. They immediately fell far behind Henry.

Henry raised his head and extended his wings to change his vertical motion to horizontal. They had never seen this before either. He went low to the ground, and headed directly toward the first light pole. The others followed, though they continued to lag far behind Henry. The four geese were trying to close the gap, but Henry was flying too fast.

As Henry approached the first pole, he rotated 90 degrees clockwise, which pushed him inches to the right side of the pole. The other geese were slower in their descent and were falling further behind. They had to start their turn sooner and traveled farther outside the pole than Henry.

They were stunned. They had never imagined that anyone could fly like Henry was flying. Thoughts that they were going to lose entered their minds for the first time, and they tried to quicken their pace.

And, so it went for a few poles. Henry held his turns tight to the poles, and the challenging team, unaccustomed to the sharp corners, was swinging out much farther than necessary, adding distance to their flight placing them further and further behind. On one pole, Henry swung tightly around it and stayed outside for an extra second to avoid the deer sign. Within a second after Henry passed the deer sign, he heard a twang, a honk, and a thud. One of the challengers had hit the deer sign. He bounced off and hit the ground hard.

Henry did not see this, as it was not a good moment to look back. If he could have looked back, he would have seen the surprised goose standing with difficulty. He slowly tested his feet, wings, and head. Once the wrecked goose felt he could fly again, he slowly and humbly, flew home. He had had enough.

The next goose had to assume the lead position behind Henry, but he closed no distance. After a couple of poles, another sign appeared. This sign was wider than the last. Henry knew, as he swung around the pole, that he also had to gain three feet of altitude, allowing him to glide over it. After he had passed the sign, there was a thud and a squawk and feathers slowly fell to the ground. The second goose had not seen the sign soon enough to avoid it. He had tried to gain altitude, but he hit it hard with his breast and ricocheted off the sign. He was shaken, but he could fly back to his home, and that is what he did.

The third goose assumed leadership. The remaining two geese rapidly approached the end of the road where Henry made an unusually sharp left turn to miss the tennis courts, and then swung again to miss a pole. The third goose had only realized he was leading his team when he saw Henry make his left turn. The third goose made a wider swing and was executing a 45-degree roll when he crashed into the tennis court fence. It squeaked as it stretched to absorb the goose's energy. Once the goose's forward motion ceased, the fence's elasticity threw the goose in the opposite direction and deposited him on the ground on his back. Henry could not see him, but he was lying quietly, resting on his back with his feet still and stretched skyward. After a moment to collect his thoughts, the third goose rolled over, tested his legs, and flew home, hoping that there had been no witnesses.

Now, only one goose remained to challenge Henry, but victory was unlikely since Henry was flying like the devil himself was behind him. He completed his turn to the left and moved inside the first pole and then outside the next pole while moving up to pass over the transparent bus stop. As he passed the bus stop, he heard another thump followed by a loud and mournful honk, and then another thump. The last goose had hit the ground. This goose was hurt seriously. He bent his beak and broke his wing. He hit the plastic wall head on. The wall was not elastic and did not absorb the goose's energy. The goose never saw it and was unable to take any evasive action, other than hitting the ground. All that remained for him to do was to slowly limp back to his home while his hurt wing hung loosely by his side and his distorted beak showed him the way.

Henry did not look back or slow down. Now, he raced against time. He felt that this might be his fastest time ever. Henry thought that the competition helped him to perform better. He turned toward the parking lot and passed over an academic building and glided smoothly onto the pond. He grinned inside and out. Henry was happy. It appeared that the first stage of the race was also the last stage. The teasing would stop.

Mother and Father Goose heard the stories circulating about the flying challenge. They went to Henry and asked him about it. Henry explained that some of the young geese were playing and that it was nothing serious. Henry offered no details. Mother and Father Goose looked at each other and exchanged silent, prideful smiles. It would have been incorrect for Henry to brag about beating other geese by using a talent provided by the Great Goose.

Each day they were more certain that Henry was special. If it would have been acceptable behavior, Mother and Father Goose would have enjoyed the humiliation of the other geese, but this was unacceptable behavior. Henry was encouraged to follow a higher standard. They were teaching Henry to be modest and to be careful not to allow his pride to cause him to misuse his special talent.

chapter

THREE

Early one morning, Henry was grazing between the classrooms and the parking lot. Fog hung heavily in the air swallowing the buildings and the trees. Sounds were amplified. When a student walked on the grass and snapped a twig, it sounded like a tree cracking under the weight of snow and ice. It was sharp, crisp, and clear. A distant student's breathing was as easily heard as if he was walking nearby.

This intersection on campus was always congested with students because it was a cross roads between the library and several classroom buildings. In spite of it being early, Henry was already walking around sniping grass blades and waiting for someone to sit on the bench and offer him some bread. Henry liked bread. People often brought bread or crackers to this spot and offered them to the geese.

Soon, a young gander joined Henry. This pleased Henry because he liked her. She appeared to like him too since she chose to graze with him. Two young male geese quickly joined them and, as geese usually do, they formed a goose line. Henry guided them around the bench area still hoping someone would appear with some bread to share with them.

Two students met on the walkway and started to talk. Since the conversation continued longer than expected, they sat on the bench. One student was doing most of the talking. Without thinking, the listening student reached down and grabbed an acorn and thoughtlessly threw it. It landed near Henry, who honked in protest. The student was oblivious to Henry as he was completely absorbed in the other student's story. His hand reached down and found another acorn, which he threw again. This time it hit the young female gander who jumped into the air, honked, and flew away in protest. Again, the student was oblivious to his discourtesy towards the geese.

Henry did not like his lady friend being treated unkindly and was annoyed because he had wanted her to stay with him. Although they were only friends, he liked her companionship. Henry looked at his two male companions and honked for them to follow him. They all squawked and honked, as they must before flying. This preflight honking is a goose's way to tell others to clear a path because take-off is imminent. If geese do not first squawk, they cannot fly, nor can they land. This habit is known well and followed by all geese.

Henry's reluctant companions were nervous because they were aware of Henry's flying capability, his love for speed, and careless moves. They also noticed that the visibility above eight feet was zero.

Henry swung them away from the buildings and remained close to the ground and under the tree branches, so they only had to miss the tree trunks. He increased his speed and turned to their left to fly between an academic building and the library. He slowly increased their altitude while honking slowly and repeatedly as he flew.

Students gazed into the sea of fog and, hearing the sound of an invisible goose honking, stopped and looked around trying to locate it. It was a magical scene. The world seemed to disappear above eight feet where the fog engulfed everything. Anyone moving higher than the fog became invisible, but Henry's honk, emitted every three seconds, was loud, clear, and confident. He knew where he was and where he was going. His friends were not as confident. In fact, they were fearful because geese do not fly at low altitudes in heavy fog through areas filled with trees and buildings. All geese knew this, but only Henry ignored it.

The honks sounded weaker as Henry and his team flew away from the bench and over the student union building. He swung them around and returned over the administrative building. He led them toward the south side of an academic building and decreased their altitude because there were many trees on its south side.

Henry's honks became louder as he approached the academic building. As the other two geese entered the fog-covered trees, they tried to avoid the branches. They fell further behind Henry, who had memorized the placement of each tree and each branch, while his companions had no idea what was in front of them. They began to honk—slowly at first, and then more and more frequently. They honked as fear turned into desperation and finally into terror. Each goose's honk was distinguishable from the other. They flew towards Henry's last honk. Henry began honking faster. Every student had stopped and was looking around trying to locate the distressed geese.

As Henry flew through the trees, the sound from one of his struggling companions was especially audible. His companion's honks became more frequent and higher in pitch, indicating anxiety. Then, Henry heard his friend hit the branches, then a squawk, and the sound of an object falling through branches, and, finally, a thud as the goose hit the ground.

Henry burst from the fog-covered trees and rose to fly around a short tree. Moments later, the second goose popped from the trees. They crossed the black asphalt ribbon connecting the parking lot to the classrooms and flew around a short tree. They made a sharp turn toward the offensive student. Henry's friend still lagged behind. The two students turned to face the geese that were quickly closing the gap between them.

The students' mouths slowly widened as they watched the geese heading directly toward their heads. They could not believe that two geese were flying straight toward them. Henry honked as a warning to the students and as a signal to his companion. Suddenly, at the moment before a collision with the student, both geese darted straight upward. The two students' heads followed the geese skyward and watched as they disappeared into the fog above their heads. Henry swung around and floated to a stop on top of the building. He jumped up on the edge of the roof and looked down in the direction of the students. He stood tall, flapped his wings to draw attention, and honked repeatedly. The other goose flew on to the pond. He wanted no more of Henry's silliness. The students could not see Henry standing on the building, but they were staring in disbelief at the fog as the goose honk was coming from the same point for several seconds.

The student, who had thrown the acorns, was still looking skyward in complete disbelief with his mouth open. Before the other student turned to walk away, she politely reminded her friend that his mouth was still open. He looked at her and then looked up toward where Henry was flapping his wings and honking.

Finally, he closed his mouth. He looked like he was going to speak, but no words left his mouth. He heard a noise from under a tree, and turning his head towards the sound, saw a goose emerging from under the trees and walking toward the pond and away from the academic building. The goose shook his head and wings as he walked. The student looked at the goose and pointed at it as he looked again for his friend, but she had already disappeared. Sounds from the goose continued as it walked toward the pond. It seemed to be talking to itself and was unhappy.

Later, when Henry returned to be with Mother and Father Goose, they had already learned of the incident. When Henry saw them, he seemed to be happy and content with himself. They were not as happy as Henry was. They started to question him about what had happened. They asked him why he had reacted as he did. Had Henry been seeking revenge on the student? Did Henry believe he was defending his lady friend? They asked Henry why he did not take his friends and leave the area. They asked Henry to explain if he thought this was the proper use of his special flying skills. If Henry had any special skills, they should not be squandered on foolish things. They urged him to be more responsible in his actions. If he were to lead other geese, he would have to be more thoughtful of the possible consequences.

Henry listened as Mother and Father Goose questioned him. He lowered his head in respect as he realized that he had acted improperly. It was clear to him that the Great Goose would not approve of his actions. After Mother and Father Goose fell silent and there was a suitable pause, Henry apologized to his Mama and Papa and admitted that, perhaps, he was showing off to the young lady, and to his two male friends. This was a good lesson for Henry: revenge is not good. Henry promised he would be more thoughtful in his actions.

The next day Henry went to an area between two academic buildings. He often found bread or crackers on the bricks near the entrance and hoped he would find some today. He located a spot where he could see everything, but where it would be difficult for people to see him.

While Henry was waiting for food, he watched people hurrying from one building to another. For the first time, he noticed the doors. He saw people approach the doors, reach out, and open them. Before they closed, two or three people entered. He looked around to determine if anyone had noticed him. When he was satisfied that he had not been noticed, he returned to watching the doors. Sometimes, people approached the doors, and they opened automatically, without anyone reaching out to touch the doors.

He was curious about what everyone did inside the building. He wanted to enter the building and see why people went there. He had forgotten about eating crackers. He could now only think about what was on the other side of the doors. Before he realized it, he was pacing back and forth as he watched the doors open and the people enter and leave the building.

Over time, Henry had developed an ability to look at people and know if they were a threat to him. Most geese survived by mistrusting all people and always keeping a safe distance between themselves and people. However, as geese and people began to share the same spaces on campus, it became necessary for geese to evaluate people. Henry observed that some people were hostile toward geese, while others were kind, and still others were indifferent.

As Henry continued to watch the door, he saw a young lady swing a door open and enter the building. Henry felt the urge to follow her into the building. Mentally, he ran to the door and passed through it before it closed. It seemed easy. The door appeared locked in the open position. Henry decided this was his chance. He looked around. Once satisfied that no one had noticed him; he boldly charged towards the door. The door started to close. Henry was hurrying and the door was closing. So far, no one had noticed Henry, even though he was surrounded by students; they were not expecting a goose walking by their side. And so it was that Henry approached the door unseen while surrounded by countless students.

It happened very quickly. When Henry was in the doorway, a cylinder snapped the door shut. Henry jumped when he felt the sharp edges of the aluminum door touch his feathers. The door caught and severed Henry's right foot at the ankle. Henry panicked. He flapped his wings violently and squawked, terrified and pained. The college student Henry was following turned around; she was so distraught by what she saw, she was incapable of taking any action. She had had no idea that Henry was following her into the building. In fact, she had not noticed any geese in the area. Blood already covered the floor and the doors. Henry was flapping around and honking loudly. He did not know what to do. His ankle burned, and the pain was unbearable; yet, he was trapped. Henry was certain he was about to die.

Another student saw what had happened and rushed to the door to open it. The first student was still frozen in disbelief with her hand over her mouth. Within seconds, in spite of his affliction, Henry saw the opened door and bolted back outside. Each step caused sharp pains to shoot throughout his body. He was no longer trapped, and when he found he could not walk on his leg, he took to flight and flew low and around the academic building toward the pond. He only thought of cooling his leg in the pond. His leg burned. He landed clumsily on the pond. When he dropped his feet to ski to a stop, his stump leg caught the water and swung him around to his right. The cool water helped to sooth the pain, but it was still excruciating.

Henry did not try to swim. He only floated. He cried because the pain was unbearable. Within minutes, Mother and Father Goose had heard about Henry's tragedy and arrived to float near him. Henry squawked loudly and constantly, as much from shock as from the pain.

Mother Goose waited a few moments for Henry to pause and then ordered him to listen to her. Henry always obeyed. Mother Goose told Henry that, though he was in great pain, he had to be silent. She asked him to think about the Great Goose and imagine his kindness and his healing power, and to visualize the Great Goose removing his pain. She told Henry to visualize each drop of blood as pain being removed by the Great Goose. Henry closed his eyes and remained silent. His mother continued to talk softly to Henry. When she tired, Father Goose continued. Together, they kept Henry calm.

They spent the night on the pond. Henry appeared to finally sleep. Mother Goose floated at his side and Father Goose floated a few yards away.

The next morning, Henry awoke to the pulsating pain starting at his stump and extending to all parts of his body. He saw Mother and Father Goose by his side and asked, "Mama, Papa, what has happened? What can I do? It hurts so much!" Henry looked at his Mama and Papa. His face could not conceal the pain he was suffering nor the confusion he felt.

Mother and Father Goose had spent the previous night talking. They had never seen a goose survive without both legs. Now, their Henry only had one leg. They had often considered the many possible fates that Henry might have, but they had never imagined this as one of them. They were frightened and perplexed. They believed, completely, that Henry had been selected by the Great Goose to do special things. Now, Henry's situation seemed hopeless. Did they not understand the Great Goose? Had the Great Goose changed His mind? Why would He allow Henry to die so young? It would be a life unfulfilled. Surely, the Great Goose could not intend Henry to serve a higher purpose and now allow him to die without the possibility of serving Him. Why would He allow this to happen? Was this an accident that the Great Goose had not foreseen, or was it one that He could not prevent? Or, was this part of the Great Goose's plan for Henry? But surely, Henry would not die! The Great Goose could not allow Henry to die! They were confused but had to remain strong to give Henry strength. They were not ready to accept Henry's demise.

Mother Goose spoke first to Henry. She said, "Henry, you must be strong. Always remember that you are a special goose. Your father and I believe that the Great Goose has given you a special purpose in life. We cannot believe that it is the Great Creator's wish that you die now. Father Goose and I believe that this is the start of His need for you. There can be no other explanation. You must stay here and, as difficult as it is, you must clear your mind. If you can, think of nothing. Ask the Great Goose to speak to you and to guide you. Since you are young and inexperienced, ask Him to speak plainly so that you cannot misunderstand. Ask Him to help you to perfectly interpret His message, to unerringly go where He wants you to go, and to impeccably do all that He wants you to do. Your father and I will stay with you until the Great Goose reveals His desire for you, as we believe He will. We are family. For now, our destiny is one." Henry looked at both of them and managed a weak smile. Father Goose honked softly to acknowledge his concurrence with Mother Goose's assessment.

This small family of geese floated for almost two days without eating. Little was said. The Great Goose and Henry's foot were never mentioned again. Occasionally, they spoke of Henry's escapades around the trees and other special moments that made them smile, but silence was the order of the day. If the Great Goose was to be heard, silence had to be maintained. They each thought of the Great Goose and asked that He save Henry and, somehow, guide him so that Henry would survive to meet his destiny.

On the third day, Henry slowly became aware that he was feeling something he had never felt before. He was like a dog that heard a distant and unfamiliar sound. He concentrated all mental energies on isolating and identifying the sounds. He could not. He remained very still, closed his eyes, and listened intently. Mother and Father Goose believed that Henry was resting and were glad, because he needed to rest.

After several hours, Henry opened his eyes and glanced about to find his Mama and Papa. When he found them, he said, "Mother, Father, I believe that the Great

Goose is speaking to me, but I am not certain. I wish I knew if it is the Great Goose speaking, or if I am hearing or imagining voices. I don't know, but I must fly northwest. I believe this is what the Great Goose wants me to do, but it seems so silly. What is happening to me?"

Mother Goose drew her Henry near and caressed his head and neck several times with her beak. Father Goose came from the other side and did the same. They told Henry they loved him. Henry asked, "Where will He take me? How will I know when I have arrived? What do I eat and how can I be safe?" Mother and Father Goose exchanged glances and Father Goose said, "Henry, place all faith in the Great Goose. He has a plan for you. All you must do is to do what He wants. Keep your mind clear and think about the Great Goose. He will provide food for you and keep you safe." Henry knew that his Mother and Father were as uncommon as they told him he was. He nuzzled each of them for a moment. Mother and Father Goose then sighed and floated away from Henry. With some difficulty, Henry squawked and jumped into the air, took flight, and circled over the pond before he set a northwest course. Mother Goose broke down and cried as though she would never see her son again. She felt her heart being ripped from her body. Father Goose used his beak to nuzzle Mother Goose's neck while he watched Henry disappear into the horizon. He also felt uncontrollable sadness.

chapter

FOUR

Henry's leg hurt. The pain was sharp and throbbing. As he flew, he was sad because he had left Mother and Father Goose and his friends and all that was familiar to him. He had no idea where he was going. He felt that he should fly in this direction, so he did. He had no experience following his intuition or the Great Goose, and he was uncertain. He continued because there was nothing else he could do.

As he flew, he tried to free his mind. He focused on the rhythm of his wings moving up and down, and then he imagined the sound of nothing.

Henry knew that if he returned to his Mama and Papa, he would die. A one-legged goose never survives long. He had to continue; so on he flew—hour after hour. The flying was difficult because the wind was brisk, and he had no lead goose to open a path for him. He was the path-breaker, and he grew tired. There were no other geese to lead the gaggle or to honk encouragement. He needed to focus his energy. He had to forget how tired he was, how hungry he was, and how much pain and loneliness he felt. He thought about Mother and Father Goose and what they might be doing at this moment. He remembered the night when they fought with the pair of coyotes and won. He remembered how they told him he was a special goose. He did not feel special. If he was special, why did he lose his leg in the door, and why was he far from home and alone now?

He thought about the Great Goose. Did he really exist? He tried again to clear his mind. Where was the Great Goose? Henry would feel better if he could see the Great Goose and if they could talk. He wanted the Great Goose to tell him what He wanted Henry to do. Henry never knew how lonely a goose without a gaggle could feel.

Henry flew on. His severed foot had stopped bleeding, but if it was bumped, the wound would reopen and the bleeding would start anew. Henry wanted to touch down on a pond, but he did not see any, and he was fearful that, if a pond did exist, there might be unfriendly inhabitants nearby. If threatened, he might not be able to react quickly enough to escape. He must stay focused and fly on. Mile after mile and hour after hour, Henry persisted. It was mind over hunger, confusion, pain, and doubt.

Henry was unaware that he had flown all the way to Nebraska and was approaching a small city located a few miles south of the Platte River. Henry would soon find relief, but he was still unaware that he was about to arrive at a small city. And of course, Henry knew nothing about this town or its history. Some say that this city is not a small city, but a large town; others simply have never given it consideration. Most people agree that the huge trees that line the broad street make cars appear small and insignificant. The houses are well kept and the lawns mowed and the people are friendly.

Like many small cities, the old central business district had been in decline for years. This had disturbed many of the people who never seemed to stop talking about it. However, to everyone's surprise, a group was formed. They started to discuss what could be done to attract new businesses, and to keep its citizens shopping at home rather than in another city.

After they talked and attended many meetings and applied for endless grants, the city had a plan...and the money to make revitalization happen, including closing the main street to cars and converting it to a pedestrian walkway. They planted beautiful trees along both sides of the street. Many of the storefronts were remodeled and made to appear more modern and attractive to shoppers.

Some said that the touch of genius to the plan had been to build a huge water fountain where the two principle streets crossed. It was much larger than anyone expected and it was expensive to build, but they hoped it would impress shoppers and convert them from occasional shoppers into repeat shoppers.

Being Nebraska, some argued that it was not a touch of genius, but madness. The city did not need a cement pond in the middle of a street. For people who wanted water, the city had a swimming pool, and the Platte River ran within a few miles of this large town, plus numerous sand pits were located all around the city. It was not necessary to build more ponds, especially with taxpayer money. However, the optimists won, and the pessimists quieted and disappeared or went underground.

Most people appeared impressed, though, there were some who continued to be against it. The naysayer's told everyone who would listen "that it was just a waste of taxpayers' hard-earned money." Business in the downtown area improved slightly, and over time, the small city's leaders seemed vindicated; however, no one expected an over night miracle. People found the sound and sight of water relaxing and refreshing. Many people stopped to sit on the edge of the fountain and found it refreshing.

chapter

FIVE

No one noticed when the gaggle first appeared. One day people saw the geese swimming in the fountain. They happily dipped their heads in and out of the water, shaking from side to side with water flying in all directions. If people listened carefully, they would hear their joyful sounds; the same sound people and dogs make when their heads are wet, and they shake them.

The farmers in the coffee shop usually talked about the weather and the price of corn and, during the fall, the University of Nebraska football team. Now, they added the geese coming to town to their conversational agenda. Even the store clerks talked with each other and with customers about the geese. Everyone was grateful to have another topic to discuss.

Then, as soon as everyone became accustomed to the geese, they disappeared. People looked at the goose-less fountain and felt emptiness. They were surprised how much the geese had become a part of their daily routines. Now, people talked about the weather, the price of corn, and the absence of the geese. Everyone always worried that it would not rain, that the price of corn would drop, and now, that the geese would not return.

One day, when the sun rose; the geese were back. People noticed that the geese had daily rituals. No one knew where they spent the night, but early in the morning the geese flew to the park and lined up to start eating. Geese do everything in an organized fashion. Sometimes their eating line is not perfect, but it is a line. As the sun rose and the temperature increased, the goose-line slowly moved towards the shade. Once there, they settled down by staking a claim to a spot of grass and lowered their bodies onto the refreshing grass where they started to pick lazily at it with their beaks. After they picked each area clean, they stood, took a few steps, and squatted again. Some stopped grazing and slept. Others picked and fussed with their feathers in the same manner that young ladies swing their hair side-to-side as they brush it.

Late in the afternoon, the geese started to assemble into one group. They were honking and fussing with their feathers and wandering around. Chaos dominated as they started to wander from here to there with no recognizable formation. Suddenly, one goose started to walk toward the fountain. It was never possible to see which goose initiated the movement. Eventually, a single line developed and the whole gaggle waddled toward the fountain. They stayed in the middle of the street, putting as much distance as possible between themselves and the people next to the store windows.

Geese were not strangers to the local citizenry; however, people were not accustomed to having geese so close to them. In this hunters' paradise, geese lived longer by keeping distance between themselves and the humans. However, even if the geese were not worried about the humans, they managed to keep a few yards between the people and themselves.

Arriving at the fountain, they fluttered onto the edge and jumped into the water. They rearranged their feathers on their backs, then, they shifted their attention to their chest and wings. When they reached back to clean their tail feathers, they started to turn in small circles. They finished their grooming by reversing direction. When they were satisfied that everything was perfect; they jumped from the water onto the fountain's edge. They stood tall and rapidly flapped their wings making a sound that was not easy to identify. Hearing this sound, shoppers and store clerks came outside and searched to find the sound's source. When they saw the geese flapping their wings at the fountain, they pointed in astonishment. The children giggled, the women smiled and the men said "By golly, would you look at that!"

The geese jumped from the fountain edge and wandered around while waiting for the others to finish the afternoon bath ceremony. Once the feathers were in place and dry, the geese started honking and milling around until one goose stepped out from the gaggle and headed toward the park. Again, the goose line formed as they departed for the park. Each goose had a place in the line. Arriving at the park, they grazed for a while before flying off to spend the night in some secret spot.

After a few weeks, shoppers began to expect the geese. One afternoon when the geese were at the fountain swimming, an old woman dug into her purse and grabbed a plastic sack containing slices of bread. She tore a slice into small pieces, and threw them into the water. The geese accepted them with enthusiasm, but they quickly taught her not to throw the bread into the water. They preferred the bread placed at the edge of the fountain where they grabbed it; dipped it into the water and then swallowed it happily. Each goose had its own technique. One goose dipped it quickly into the water while another dragged it back and forth until it melted in his mouth.

Older people learned to visit the fountain with bread at this time of day and the geese would always be waiting. The geese were always appreciative and fought for the best position in the fountain. There was pushing and shoving and honking, tail feathers were pulled and behinds bitten, all to the delight of the visitors. The geese made the senior citizens feel important. Some could not remember the last time anybody fought for their attention...even if it was just geese.

The geese were peaceful and did not interfere with any of the businesses or shoppers. But, one small problem soon became apparent—when the geese traveled in formation between their two favorite locations, they left droppings. It was inevitable. Geese did not know people-etiquette. To understand the dimensions of the problem, a large goose can drop four pounds of wet material a day.

To most people, it was not a problem since the geese waddled in straight lines and always used the same path, but there were a few people who resented the geese. The Frisbee players in the park had to be careful when they dived for their Frisbee before it hit the ground. Even people who walked their dogs sometimes complained, but theirs was not an aggressive voice; they were walking dogs that were also not knowledgeable about people-etiquette and often made their deposits in the park.

Many people who complained about the droppings were the same people who had been against the taxpayers' money being spent on a useless fountain that the geese had confiscated for their own use. Their argument was that the geese had the entire Platte River; they did not need a fountain. The ladies with open-toe high heels and anyone with sandals had to pay attention where they put their feet. Every time a goose hunter had to side-step, his thoughts turned to the next hunting season. Even some non-hunters considered starting to hunt. Others were not concerned about waiting for the official hunting season to open.

The city government took these complaints seriously and a new part-time job opened. It involved a small cart on wheels which held a small wastebasket lined with a plastic bag. A high school student waited for the parade to form at the park each afternoon and followed it from a respectful distance, removing all remnants. The same process was repeated later, only it started at the fountain and ended at the park. Most people were happy with this solution, but a few still counted the days until goose hunt-ing season started.

People became so acquainted with the individual geese that they were able to determine that a hierarchy existed, and that the order of the geese in their parade line represented their social status within the gaggle.

chapter

SIX

Henry was tired and hungry and miserable; he could fly no further. He looked down and saw a pond in the middle of the town. It was not large, but it was a pond. He made his decision and started a fast descent. He flew around from east to west and proceeded down the main street at head level. As he passed in front of stores, store workers and shoppers were surprised when they saw a lone goose glide by. This was unusual because the resident gaggle had already taken their dip in the fountain and paraded to the park and then disappeared to their secret resting place. People recognized this lone goose flying by as an unusual event because the resident gaggle never flew down Main Street; they paraded.

Henry splashed down in the fountain and felt the wonderful cool water on his foot. He allowed his body to relax and he drank heartily from the fountain, but he was hungry. He was extremely hungry. It had been three days since he last ate. To stop thinking about his hunger, and his precarious situation, he focused his mind on the Great Goose. As he concentrated, he felt Him entering his mind and slowly passing through his body. It was a warm, tingling sensation. Finally, it left through his missing foot, and with it, the pain disappeared. Henry closed his eyes and opened his mind and asked the Great Goose to speak to him, to give him some sign that he was on the right trail. Henry was not confident. He had no experience being on his own. It was not natural for a goose to be alone, although Henry was on a quest; he did not know what the quest was. He had no idea what he was doing

Henry floated on the pond. Several times he dipped his head into the water and pulled it out and shook his head back and forth to cast off the water. He liked to feel the coolness of the water flying from his head. When he tried to paddle, however, he found that he went in small circles since he had only one paddle. This annoyed Henry. To help, he tried to move his good leg further under his body to compensate for the missing one. He still swam in a circular motion but, at least, it was a wider circle.

Henry's body reminded him that he was still tired and hungry. He had no idea what to do for food. He could not walk on his stump. He could fly, but he did not know where to fly. Safety was his primary consideration. The world did not forgive careless geese. They disappeared quickly. He did not know where he could safely spend the night, but he thought the fountain might be safer than any other place. He would have a few seconds warning if anyone, or anything, approached the fountain.

The store located on the southeast corner from the fountain was a shoe repair shop. It was not prosperous and showed its age in the old and dingy curtains and cracked paint on the outside. Today, most people throw away worn shoes and buy another pair. It is no longer common to repair shoes. The only people who send their shoes for repair are older people who grew up during the Depression, or the Second World War. It was normal not to have many clothes. What clothes they owned had to be recycled, again and again, because no one knew when new ones could be bought. The shoe repair clientele was rapidly declining. Each year the Depression and World War II people were a year older and walked less and there were fewer of them.

The Cobbler appeared in the front window and peered under a half-pulled shade to gaze into the street at nothing in particular, as he often did when he needed to stand and stretch his body. His appearance revealed that he was near retirement age. His thick graying hair was very short, though his hairline was retreating some. His face was wrinkled, and he wore a pair of eyeglasses with half-moon lenses. He always had an old and dirty apron covered with black and brown stains from polishing and shining shoes. He wiped his hands on his apron as he stared blankly out the window. Each hour he stood from his bench and walked to the window to stretch his back and shoulders, though he was going to see nothing in particular, he always looked out the window.

The Cobbler started to turn toward his workbench when his eye caught a glimpse of something that was out of place. He stopped and turned back toward the fountain for a second look and was amused by a lone goose dipping his head into the pond, pulling it out, and shaking it furiously. When the water stopped flying, the goose dipped his head again into the water, pulled it out, and flung water everywhere again. He was not a member of the town gaggle because it had already left for the evening, and they always traveled as a group.

The Cobbler went to his door, opened it, and stepped outside. He put his hands on his hips and watched Henry. Since Henry was still playing in the water, he had not yet noticed the Cobbler observing him. The Cobbler stepped closer to Henry and stopped. Then, he slowly took another step and stopped again. Now, Henry sensed he was being watched and positioned himself to keep an eye on the Cobbler. He did not look directly at the Cobbler, but he saw every move the Cobbler made. The Cobbler watched Henry, and Henry obliquely watched the Cobbler. When the Cobbler took another step, Henry turned to look directly at him. Their eyes met and locked onto each other. Henry was telling the Cobbler that he should not come closer to Henry. The Cobbler, wishing to test Henry, slowly took another step. Henry's head rose slightly. Their mutual gaze intensified. They were studying each other. The Cobbler took another step. Henry's body became rigid, and he followed the Cobbler's every move.

Henry's heart accelerated as he considered his alternatives. He did not like anyone coming so close to him, especially now that he was missing a leg; however, he was tired and did not want to fly away. He needed to hold his ground and rest. He wanted the Cobbler to leave, but the Cobbler persisted, and took more steps. Henry watched. He studied this human's eyes and subtle body movements. Henry squawked and tried back paddling when the Cobbler came within a few steps of touching Henry. The Cobbler froze, noticing Henry's problem paddling. The Cobbler took a few steps back, and then he spoke softly, "That's ok, fella. Where are your friends? You look like you're alone. It's no fun being alone, is it? You have a problem with your foot, eh fella? I wonder if you would let me look at it." He took more steps back. Henry continued to watch every movement. When the Cobbler reached his door, he re-entered the store. He pulled the "Closed" sign down, pulled the shades, and disappeared.

Within 20 minutes from the time the Cobbler disappeared, he reappeared with a bucket in his hand. He took a few steps toward the fountain and stopped. He said, "Well, fella, I've got some delicious Nebraska corn for you. If you let me, I'll put some on the edge of the fountain. Will you let me?" Henry stared at the Cobbler. The Cobbler took another step.

The Cobbler approached the fountain slowly. Henry floated to the opposite side to maintain a safe distance. The Cobbler reached the fountain edge and poured some corn on it. Before leaving, he said, "Now eat that and you'll feel better. Maybe I'll see you tomorrow. I can return early and give you more corn, if you can wait that long. Goodnight, you big handsome guy. I wonder where you've come from and what stories you could tell." With that, he backed away slowly and re-entered his shop.

Henry did not wait long to approach the corn. He ate quickly. In fact, he devoured the corn. The corn was excellent and slowly his hunger disappeared, but now his exhaustion surfaced. He floated to the center of the fountain and rested. Tomorrow, he decided, he would explore the park.

Very early the next morning, the Cobbler reappeared with more corn. Henry accepted and ate it leaving no kernels behind. The Cobbler returned to his store and watched from the window. Henry ate, but watched the Cobbler as he ate. When he finished, Henry looked toward the park and jumped into the air.

Henry stayed close to the ground while he flew toward the park. He landed in the shade of a tree, but the landing was not an easy one. He tried to land with most of his weight on his good foot to protect his stump from impact. When he hit the ground, he had to take a few steps to avoid falling. His stump renewed its bleeding and again pain shot through his body. Finally, he settled on the grass and ate. With his long neck he could eat around his body. When all the choice grass was gone, he fluttered his wings to take himself to a new position a few feet away and repeated the process. It was slow and painful; but, thanks to the Cobbler, Henry did not need much food. He mostly needed to rest.

In the next several days, Henry started to trust the Cobbler, who was always respectful of Henry. Henry allowed the Cobbler to approach closer each day. Finally, the Cobbler sat a few feet away as Henry ate. Henry never took his eyes off the Cobbler, but soon realized he was not a threat. In fact, Henry felt he had found a new friend and felt more comfortable in the Cobbler's presence. This was strange, but Henry began to feel that they could trust each other.

The Cobbler, though a part of his community for 40 years and known by all, was not well-known by anyone. He was always working, and when people entered his shop, he was always courteous and kind but he was not a person who attracted others. He was a loner and not frequently approached by anyone. No one invited him for a holiday celebration or bought him a drink or even thought about him. There was always an invisible barrier present. He co-existed with the world, but he was not a part of it. Strangely, the Cobbler did not want to be a part of it. He was like a drop of oil floating on water. He did not long to be anyone else or anything else. He was what he was, and that is what he wanted.

The citizens of the small city also did not know that the Cobbler was a Marine or that he had fought in the Korean War. He came from a farm in another state and settled here because no one knew him, and he had no other place to go. No one in the community knew, or gave any thought to, the origin of the Cobbler. There were no questions that seemed to tickle peoples' minds about the Cobbler. The Cobbler simply was.

When he was young, he found school difficult and not to his liking. He abandoned it when he was 16 years old and obtained a job for three or four years helping a cobbler. It suited him. He was good working with his hands and his father's farm was not large enough to support more people, so that was not an option.

When the Korean War started, he joined the Marines. He left home, but few people noticed. His mother and father were very humble people, and no one noticed his absence except his family.

The government, in extreme need of troop reinforcements, abbreviated the company's training, and within weeks, the Cobbler was in Korea facing combat. Initially, his company was optimistic and certain that the war would end quickly. It did not. Instead, they were pushed south until they were isolated, and their destiny did not appear a happy one. Then, General McArthur landed near Seoul, Korea and alleviated the pressure on the Cobbler's company.

They started north, reached Seoul, and began to continue north. They quickly moved along the east coast of Korea. The enemy appeared to be melting as they approached. The army troops and the Marines moved rapidly to the north. The army leaders told everyone to move quickly to the north. They had to keep driving the enemy and keep them in disarray, even if their own supply lines were thin to non-existent. The Marine leader, a cautious and practical man, refused to accelerate the movement of his Marines beyond their supplies. He was not popular among other military leaders, but this did not change his leadership. He knew that the war would be won by men. He did not have many, but those who were still alive, were not going to be lost due to his foolishness.

The rest was history. Enemy troops burst over the border from the north and crushed the U.S. army with their overwhelming numbers and surprise. The Marines moved south. Winter broke loose and was viciously and unrelentingly cold. Most soldiers and Marines did not have the appropriate clothing and froze. They quickly suffered shortages of ammunition and weapons.

Many soldiers and Marines died. They were wounded and had no medical supplies. They had no ammunition and were freezing. They had to fight while retreating, and the enemy was taking no prisoners. The enemy never stopped to rest, to eat, or to sleep. They shot or bayoneted all soldiers they overtook.

The Cobbler was in the middle of this. He spent more than one year witnessing and participating in things that no human should see or do. He saw wounded and dead soldiers without legs, without arms, and without faces. He saw them burned, severely wounded, and dead. Soldiers cried for their mothers and they cried from the pain. His mind recorded their cries for help and the horrible smells. They knew they were dying. He could not forget the pungent smells of the war and death. The Cobbler did not fear hell, because he had seen something much worse. At the time, he was only 21 years old.

When he was released from the Marines and sent home, no one suspected that he would later have problems. He seldom slept. Often, he awoke screaming and crying as his mind vividly replayed the war. He learned to scream inward. He did not want his neighbors to hear his restless nights. He never married, because he feared he could not maintain a relationship. His wife would not be able to understand, he thought. It would be unfair of him to bring a wife into his life, where the war still continued each day in his mind. Even in a cold room, he would sweat and shout names and warnings to his fallen friends, as if he were still in Korea. Each night he saw their danger, but he could never save them. He would then sob uncontrollably.

The first time he reached out to anyone was the day he saw Henry. There was something about Henry that touched his soul. He looked deeply into Henry's eyes and found a kindred soul looking back. Someone needed help, and the Cobbler could help him. Now, the Cobbler thought constantly about Henry.

Most local people knew that Henry was not a member of the gaggle because he was never part of the string of geese that paraded back and forth between the park and the fountain. Walking was difficult for Henry, so he always traveled by flying very close to the ground. He chose shaded, grassy areas close to those used by the gaggle. Henry watched the gaggle like he was interested in joining, but if geese extend invitations to others to join their group, none was extended to Henry. And so, he was alone.

After several days of Henry's watching the gaggle moving about, he started following them at a respectful distance. He did not want them to think he had joined their gaggle uninvited; yet, it gave him some pleasure to walk in the line with them. When the gaggle arrived at the fountain, Henry remained behind to allow them to enter and bathe and then to dry themselves leisurely. When the gaggle returned to the park, Henry took his turn at the fountain and waited for the Cobbler's twice daily visit with corn.

Eventually, Henry tried to walk between the park and the fountain by following the gaggle. People noticed that one goose was always several feet behind the last one in the wavy procession. He had trouble keeping pace with the others. When each step was marked by a spot of blood on the sidewalk, people realized that Henry was limping. If the goose in front was the head of the gaggle, then Henry was the rear.

Most people loved the geese, but when the gimpy goose appeared, they always paid special attention to him. People went out of their way to feed Henry. He had a difficult life, they thought, and the other geese seemed to not like him. If Henry came too close to the gaggle, one of them would flutter its wings and lower its head into the attack position and hiss until Henry backed off to a more respectable position.

Everyone imagined Henry to be sad and withdrawn, but he always tried to be in the middle of things, even if he continued on the edge of things. Henry never stopped trying. People loved to watch Henry. The first person to spot the geese parade forming each day announced it to the others. People rushed to the store windows and doors and waited for the long line of geese, and finally, Henry, several feet behind the others, struggling to keep pace walking on his stump. They smiled with respect, and yet, people were sad about how difficult they imagined Henry's life was. Henry had entered their lives only a few weeks ago, and made it better. Henry's disability helped people to smile and talk to each other.

The Cobbler continued to feed Henry corn. He taught Henry to go to his back door where he could give Henry corn without attracting the attention of people or birds. The Cobbler turned a five-gallon can over and sat on it while he watched Henry eat. The Cobbler always talked softly with Henry, who became accustomed to this ritual. Even though Henry always looked obliquely at the Cobbler, the Cobbler knew he was listening. The Cobbler talked to Henry about the friends who had not returned from Korea. He explained how he could not stop thinking about them. It was not that he wanted to forget about them, but they both deserved peace now. What troubled the Cobbler most was that the difference between who lived and who died had been decided by inches, or by a split-second, or events that were unexplainable—unfair. He continually relived these horrible experiences where he tried to do something differently hoping that the outcome would be better; but it was always the same. He felt guilty that he had never been able to save many of his friends.

As the Cobbler spoke to Henry, an idea began to evolve in his mind. Each day he studied Henry's foot and watched Henry struggling to keep pace with the gaggle. His mind began to focus on Henry's foot. He began to take photographs of Henry walking. Since many people took photographs of Henry, no one noticed, especially since most of the photographs were taken as Henry ate in the privacy of the Cobbler's back door. He finally captured a likely representation of Henry's stump and obtained measurements from the photograph. He studied several pieces of leather for their wearing ability and flexibility and how closely they could simulate a goose's foot.

The Cobbler lived in the back of his store so no one knew if the Cobbler worked late or not. He closed the front door and pulled the shades, which was unusual in a small Nebraska city. He now left the back door open and worked near it. He studied Henry's photographs and thought. Sometimes, Henry lingered by the door after he finished eating, and the Cobbler would work while talking to Henry. Henry would settle to the ground and seemed to understand every word the Cobbler spoke, and the Cobbler spoke to Henry of things that he had remembered nightly for 50 years but about which he had never spoken to another human being.

He created several designs for Henry's foot. He studied how an artificial foot could attach to Henry's stump. He simulated how it would move when Henry walked, swam or flew. He smiled slightly when he thought of Henry's surprise when he realized he could again walk without limping or hurting his stump. At least, he thought he smiled. He was once asked by a young lady why he never smiled. This surprised him because he thought he often smiled. Later, when he was alone, he went to a mirror. Without looking into the mirror he made what he thought was a smile, and he turned to face the mirror. He was stunned. It was true. He was not smiling! He thought he had been smiling, but there was no smile in the mirror. Somehow, the smile was lost between his mind, his heart, and the mirror. He wondered when he had smiled for the last time.

The Cobbler worried about how the adaptive leg would react to being wet, and then dry, and then wet again. He worried about keeping it attached to Henry's stump while Henry was in flight. He feared that it might interfere with Henry's ability to fly, or would make it more difficult for Henry to keep pace with the gaggle. He worried about sores that could develop at the contact point between

Henry's stump and the adaptive foot, a result worse than only having the stump because it could become infected.

This project was more complex than he had imagined. Sometimes he was close to quitting, but twice a day, every day, Henry passed by his window on parade with the other geese, and he was always the last goose in the gaggle. Henry did not quit, so neither would the Cobbler. The Cobbler ordered samples of a special synthetic material that was rarely used by Cobblers and was very expensive.

His suppliers asked the Cobbler questions about why he was ordering these unusual materials. The Cobbler gave no information and changed the subject. Soon they stopped asking questions. They gave him what he requested. The Cobbler did not reveal to anyone details about his life or what he was doing. He was not secretive, but found that he spent most of his life alone among people.

One night Henry was eating his corn and the Cobbler decided to explain the adaptive device he was making to him. It was strange because Henry did not take his eyes from his corn while the Cobbler demonstrated the adaptive device in the air. He showed Henry how he would attach it, and how it would function when he walked, but Henry continued eating, unimpressed, yet the Cobbler knew he was aware of every detail.

The next day, during the twice-daily walk someone shouted, "Look at that goose! He has something on his foot! Look! He isn't limping any more! He has a white foot!" It was true. Henry was not limping, and he had a white foot. Where he only had a stump, Henry had a new white boot! It had the shape of his normal foot, but it was white.

The word spread fast. People came from miles around to see Henry with his white artificial foot. Newspapers placed feature articles about Henry, some with photographs. It started in the local paper and spread. The two largest newspapers in Nebraska carried impressive articles on Henry. Soon, other newspapers arrived to do stories on Henry. One was from Kansas City, another from St. Louis, and another from Chicago. One representative arrived from France and still another arrived from Japan! The citizens of this small city were as proud of Henry as they were of the Nebraska football team.

The gaggle noticed also because Henry's place in the line started to change. The goose walking in front of Henry, the last one in the normal gaggle line, allowed him to approach closer and, finally, he hesitated allowing Henry to walk in front of him. The next goose also slowed and allowed Henry to move ahead of him, and slowly, his place in the line moved closer to the front. Then it happened. One day, Henry led the gaggle down Main Street. When people saw this, word spread faster than a prairie fire on a hot, windy spring day. People filled the street, as if a parade had suddenly appeared. People talked loudly to each other and shouted for joy, as Henry made his inaugural regal appearance as the gaggle's leader.

The people did not clap because, though the geese were accustomed to people, geese still instinctively associated a clap to a shotgun blast, and would disappear in the blink of an eye. The geese were appreciated in less noisy ways, out of respect for the geese's natural instincts.

The geese were guests that were very welcome and their hosts did everything to keep them returning. No one could imagine what their town would be like now without them.

The Cobbler never admitted to being the person who built the artificial foot for Henry. Many people suspected him, and some directly asked him, but it meant more to him to be silent about it. He wanted to help Henry and he did not want any publicity. He enjoyed his role as the invisible man—the man no one saw or thought about. When asked, he would shrug his shoulders and speak of "God's mysterious ways."

As fall approached, to prevent the cold from seeping in and making customers uncomfortable, the shop owners no longer left their doors open during business hours. The Cobbler also shut his door to keep the warmth inside. One day, the Cobbler heard a repeating thud. He looked around, but did not see anything. Again, he heard the noise. He stood up and looked, and to his surprise, he saw a goose at his front door looking into the store through the door's glass pane. The goose was pecking at the pane. The Cobbler went to the door and opened it. To his surprise, the goose did not flee. Instead, he took a couple of steps inside. At first, the cobbler thought that Henry had returned for some adjustments in his new foot, but it was not Henry.

The goose looked up at the Cobbler and honked repeatedly in soft, purposeful honks. The Cobbler had no idea what the goose wanted. Then the goose picked up his right foot and pushed it out toward the Cobbler. The Cobbler saw nothing wrong with the foot. The goose then pointed at it with his right wing, and he honked again. The Cobbler was confused, until he recognized the goose as the former leader of the gaggle, the one displaced by Henry. Not knowing what to do, the Cobbler shooed the goose back out the door, but later, he wondered what the goose had wanted.

The Cobbler could not shake the experience. He asked himself, "Is it possible that the goose wanted a white boot like Henry's? Is it possible that he associated the white boot with Henry's rise to power and his own lack of a white boot with his fall from power? Do geese have power struggles? How did the goose know that he, the Cobbler, had made the shoe for Henry?"

The Cobbler was tired. He closed the store and walked into the back to relax. He never shared this experience with anyone. He did not want anyone to know what he did for Henry nor did not want people to laugh at him. Geese do not knock on doors and order white boots.

chapter

SEVEN

As the days passed, for reasons unknown to Henry, he developed a strange feeling in his stomach. At first he did not know what it meant. It was a feeling that started somewhere deep within him and made him uncomfortable. Each day the feeling moved to another place and confused Henry. He longed to speak to Mother and Father Goose, but he was alone and had to figure this out by himself. He went to the fountain while the gaggle was at the park and sat quietly and thought about the Great Goose. He asked the Great Goose, if He was trying to speak with him, to make the message clear. Slowly, ever so slowly, the feeling developed into an urge that grew stronger each day.

It was now undeniably strong. He was convinced that the Great Goose needed him somewhere. He had to start his trip. He did not know where he was going, nor why; but, he knew the Great Goose wanted him somewhere else.

He told his friends that he would leave in a few days. They could not understand why he needed to leave, especially when he did not know where he was going. Normal geese did not do this. They tried to make Henry reconsider his decision, but he would not. The pull was too strong. He was like a fish hooked on a line with a fisherman pulling at the other end. Henry had to follow the pull of the line, wherever it took him.

He ate as much as he could, knowing he would need all the energy he could manage, since flying alone took more energy than flying in a gaggle.

The last night Henry watched the Cobbler from the street. When it was late, he drifted toward the Cobbler's back door and pecked three times on the glass. The Cobbler hurried to answer the door. He smiled when he looked down and saw Henry looking up. The Cobbler opened the door and Henry entered. They went into the back room. The Cobbler sat on an old wooden chair. Henry approached and settled to the floor. The Cobbler removed the artificial leg and examined it carefully. Henry waited. The Cobbler scraped and cleaned the inside of the leg.

After a few moments, the Cobbler said something to Henry, stood up and took a few steps. He returned and placed a handful of corn on the floor for Henry. The Cobbler sat again and continued his labor and his talking.

If anyone had looked through the window at that moment, they would have seen a strange sight: an old and normally quiet and reserved man, talking easily to a goose that ate corn while sitting on the floor in front of the Cobbler. And the Cobbler was smiling; although, he was not aware of it. No one had ever seen the Cobbler with a smile. It was a special moment for both of them. There was little for the Cobbler to do because the white boot was in excellent condition. The value of the moment was that the two friends were together. Somehow the Cobbler knew that Henry was leaving and was sad, but he carried his part of the conversation. As an after thought, he grabbed a marker and very carefully inscribed his phone number on Henry's white boot. He took care to write slowly with a steady hand so that the numbers could be easily read by anyone.

After a few moments the corn disappeared, and Henry looked up. The Cobbler looked down and knew it was time. He replaced Henry's white boot. Henry took a few practice steps, looked at the Cobbler, gave an approving honk and waddled toward the door. The Cobbler followed and opened the door. Henry turned toward the Cobbler and honked affectionately, then walked out. The Cobbler watched and wondered where Henry might be going. The Cobbler was very sad because he had come to rely on his conversations with Henry. Henry was his best friend, a perfect friend that always listened, never criticized, and always maintained secrets safe.

Henry returned to his sleeping place but could not sleep. He thought about Mother and Father Goose and his friends at home. He thought about his new friends, and especially his human friend, the man who gave him back his foot, took away his pain, and fed him. He did not want to leave, but he knew the Great Goose needed him.

Henry was more comfortable following his intuition now. He was very unsure of himself during his trip from his home to Nebraska. Now, he had some confidence. If he could come to Nebraska, he could do much more.

The sun appeared on the horizon, as it always did, but it was different today because Henry did not walk to the fountain to swim. He squawked a few times and honked a few times, and others from the gaggle answered with honks of encouragement. He jumped into the air and headed west.

He gained altitude and headed north to the Platte River, and then turned upstream. Henry would follow the Platte River west. Parallel to the river was Interstate Highway 80. Generally, the river had pastures next to it due to the occasional flooding of the Platte. The sandy soil made many crops unattractive. With the land not being cultivated, trees filled the area because of the abundant water, but the most common were Cottonwood and Cedar trees.

Henry flew many hours a day because the will of the wind demanded it. He flew alone and against the wind. He was always the lead flyer and could not trade off with other geese and no one honked encouragement for him to fly strong and to fly straight. For strength, Henry thought of Mother and Father Goose and the Great Goose.

As he continued his flight west, he watched the river. It was beautiful with its large sand bars and islands, each with brush and trees. The river's edges were filled with tall grass, trees, and brush. It provided a perfect environment for geese to hide and find food.

Henry also noticed the two ribbons of vehicles, which paralleled the river. He noticed that the vehicles flew much faster than he, except when they entered the highway. He saw that the huge trucks entered the highway at very slow speeds. By the time they merged onto the interstate they were flying at the speed he flew, and then they quickly left him behind as they accelerated into the horizon. Geese can only fly 30 to 40 miles per hour.

Henry wondered if he could make faster time if he flew in front of the trucks. If he braced his feet on the front of the truck, perhaps the truck would push him west. All he would have to do would be to stay awake and keep his wings extended.

He decided to test his idea. He saw a truck approaching the on-ramp, and he circled around to merge with it as it entered the interstate. The driver watched in his left mirror for traffic as he merged into the outside lane. At the same time, Henry merged with the truck. The driver did not see Henry because, for this, he needed to look in his right mirror. Henry flew low and in front of the truck. Once there, he adjusted his elevation and waited for the truck to overtake him. He felt the air pressure change as the truck came closer to him. Finally, he felt the truck's grill touch his feet and its pressure increased. With his wings fully extended; he flew like he had never flown before; yet, he was not flapping his wings. Henry was delighted with the sensation.

The driver could not see Henry over his huge hood. Henry was gliding. It felt amazing to fly at two or three times his usually speed. The trees and posts were a blur. Soon, he felt that his feet were tiring. The truck was pushing him through the air at 80 miles per hour, and his feet had to absorb that force.

A car approached in the passing lane and slowly crept past the truck and Henry. The man driving the car had his eyes focused on the horizon. He had been driving for hours and was in a driver's trance such that he looked neither right nor left. He stayed in the passing lane and drove. A woman sat next to him and was flipping the pages of a magazine. A little girl sat in the back seat and gazed about, focusing on nothing in particular, until she saw Henry.

She looked at Henry at the same instant that Henry looked at her. Surprised, Henry smiled widely. The little girl smiled back. Then, the little girl poked her mother in the back. The mother turned to look at her daughter. The daughter spoke while pointing at Henry. Her mother shifted her weight and now turned to her right and looked. She saw Henry seemingly attached to the truck's hood, like a hood ornament. Henry smiled broadly for the mother. The lady's mouth dropped as she tried to make sense of what she was seeing. As her brain tried to understand, and could not; she screamed. The car driver glanced to his right. This motion caused the car to lurch halfway into the truck's lane. The car driver panicked at the sudden intrusion into his trance. He thought he saw a smiling goose attached to a truck hood, but was unsure because he needed to remove the car from the truck's path. To compensate, he quickly jerked the car left and out of the truck's path. The mother locked her hands onto each side of her seat so tightly that her knuckles were white.

The little girl had turned around in the seat and was looking back at Henry, waving happily.

The truck driver was always annoyed by civilian drivers who insisted on driving alongside him. It was a dangerous position. If they wanted to pass him, they should pass. Otherwise, they should stay in the travel lane behind him and keep the passing lane open. The trucker had been very annoyed by this car driver because he had been accompanying the truck in the danger zone for miles. The truck driver had been watching the car carefully when he noticed the little girl in the car looking at the front of his truck and pointing, and then the mother turned to look at the front of his truck. The truck driver looked down over the huge hood and saw nothing. Then the car jerked in front of his truck causing the potential for a very serious accident. This annoyed the truck driver more; and he instinctively reached up and gave his horn three short blasts to warn the car driver.

The car driver was not expecting to see Henry when he looked where his wife was pointing, and he was not expecting to hear the powerful truck horn in his ear. This almost caused him to lose control of the car when he overcompensated to escape from the truck. The sudden blast discombobulated Henry because he had never heard such a deafening sound. This distraction caused him to lose his footing. He relaxed his foot muscles and the truck bumped his bottom and the air draft passing over the hood pulled him higher and higher on the grill. The truck driver suddenly saw Henry and froze in disbelief. When Henry reached the top of the hood, the draft forced him back towards the windshield where he instinctively extended his feet and was moving them in a running motion until he hit the windshield wipers. He momentarily stabilized himself against the strong draft, but not before he soiled himself. Actually, he did not soil himself. He soiled the truck's windshield.

The truck driver realized that he had a car a few feet ahead of him, a goose on his windshield wipers, and goose poop on his windshield. He could not see and tried to reposition his head but all he could see was a dirty windshield and a flying goose. He turned on the windshield wipers, which only smeared his windshield making it impossible to see anything. When the windshield wipers moved up they launched Henry up and over the truck in an unpredictable path like a piece of paper or a plastic bag.

The truck driver hit the brakes. The brakes locked. The car pulled away from the truck but the truck jackknifed, taking up both lanes as it screeched sideways down the pavement. Henry was thrown tail over beak, but recovered his composure and headed towards the Platte River. He had had enough flying for one day.

The truck slowed as it slid. The noise was horrible—frozen tires on the concrete and the trailer creaking in ways the driver had never heard before. Finally, the truck stopped. It completely blocked the highway's two lanes causing traffic to stop and vehicles to accumulate behind the truck. Someone in a car behind him notified the police.

The truck driver sat a moment, frozen in his seat. His mind had not yet grasped what had happened. He unbuckled himself, turned off the engine, and climbed down. He walked in front of the truck and looked. As he examined his truck, his mind was processing what had happened. He had walked back and was looking at his trailer when he heard the approaching sirens. He now considered what he was going to say.

The highway patrol officer arrived and was walking toward the truck driver as he prepared his clip board for filling in the report. The patrolman was very serious and courteous, as they always are. He asked if anyone was hurt. Then, he asked what happened. The truck driver explained how the car had been slowly passing him, and then suddenly moved into his lane. He honked a warning to the car driver to keep him from colliding with his truck. Then a goose floated over his hood and became entangled in his windshield wipers and pooped on his windshield, obscuring his vision. The car had only been a few feet in front of him, so he applied his brakes to avoid hitting it. The brakes locked. The car continued on its way, as did the goose. Yes, there was one more thing. It had happened very quickly, but he thought he had noticed that the goose had one black foot and one white foot.

As soon as the truck driver said the last part, he realized that maybe he had provided too much information to the patrolman. The officer had listened intently to his story. He seemed interested, even entertained at the uncommonness of the story, but the truck driver noticed that his expression changed immediately when he mentioned the goose's different colored feet. The truck driver was certain that the patrolman did not believe him. When he finished telling the story, the patrolman asked him how many hours he had been driving. The truck driver answered that he was under his limit. The officer asked to see his log. The truck driver showed it to him. The patrolman asked the truck driver to wait for a moment.

The patrolman returned to his patrol car and radioed headquarters. Both the patrolman and headquarters could not put their finger on what it was, but the story seemed strange. Finally, headquarters told the officer to have the truck driver follow him to the next off ramp. They would meet him there and do some drug tests.

The officer returned to the truck driver and told him to follow to the next exit where they needed to do some tests. He asked if the truck could be moved. The driver started the engine and found all systems working. The driver asked how long he might be detained because he was trying to finish his run and return home. He had two young daughters that he had promised he would be home that night. The officer was unimpressed and motioned for the truck driver to follow his car.

Henry landed on the Platte River and found a spot to safely spend the night. He continued to think about his ride on the truck. He did not know how long he had flown, but it was the most exciting event of his life. Even so, he decided he would complete his trip the traditional way.

He found a nice place and swam before eating. He liked to dip his head into the water and then shake the excess water from his head. He liked to bathe and groom himself every day. It relaxed him, but today Henry felt that eyes were upon him. He looked around but he could not find them. He was nervous. He climbed from the water and settled into a place where he felt safe. He listened to the sounds and found nothing unusual. Slowly, he relaxed and closed his eyes. He rested and was almost asleep. Perhaps he was dreaming, but he heard a faint voice uttering, "Hello, friend. How are you?" Henry cautiously opened his eyes and looked around, but saw nothing. He tried to sleep, but he heard it again, "Hello, friend. How are you?"

Henry opened his eyes again, but still he saw nothing. Tired of this game, Henry commanded, "Who are you? Show yourself because this game is tiring." A few blades of grass moved and a head appeared. Henry, surprised, asked, "What are you? You certainly are not a goose?"

The bird stepped from the grass and answered, "I am a homing pigeon."

Henry answered, "There is no need to be ashamed of being homely, because many birds are, but what are you?"

The pigeon took two more tiny steps towards Henry and said, "My name is Anthony. I am a homing pigeon. We are known for being able to always find our home, no matter where we go. That is why we are called 'homing' pigeons. We can always find our way home. Except that, now, I cannot. I cannot find my home."

Henry asked, "Can't all birds find their way home? I certainly can."

Anthony replied that most birds he knew, who were not pigeons, could not find their way home. In fact, Anthony explained that most birds he knew were not very smart at all.

"Mr. Anthony, why are you here by the river?" asked Henry.

Anthony did not respond immediately. Finally, he said, "Because I am lost. I have been trying to find my way home for many days, and I cannot find it. I am very ashamed. My master took me many miles in a new direction. We passed over mountains and valleys, and he released me. There was a storm, a very bad storm with much wind, lightening and thunder. I tried to fly throw it but I could not. I remember I was flying and then I woke up near here and the storm was over. And now I have no idea where I am. My master will have already forgotten about me. I do not know how to defend myself here. I am small and have many enemies. I would like your protection for this evening. Perhaps we could help to defend each other," he added to make the offer more attractive. "We are stronger together than we are separately." At this, Anthony paused and studied Henry for the effectiveness of his plea.

Henry thought Anthony's story was sad and thought him harmless. Henry agreed to allow Anthony to stay with him. Anthony hesitantly approached Henry, who extended one wing, and after Anthony slid inside the pocket; Henry relaxed his wing over Anthony. No one could reach Anthony without first passing through Henry. They both slept, but Henry was more alert during sleep since he had more responsibility now. He not only had to protect himself, but he had to protect Anthony. He remembered how Father and Mother Goose had heroically defended him against the pair of coyotes. Henry felt proud to have the additional responsibility.

The next morning Henry asked Anthony what he was going to do now. Anthony had no idea, but he knew that his life span would be short if he remained alone. Henry knew this also, so he asked if Anthony would consider joining him on his flight. Anthony asked Henry where he was going. Henry still did not know. He only pointed his beak and followed it. He suggested that Anthony could fly in his draft, which would be easier for the homing pigeon. Anthony did not ask questions. He longed for a companion and needed someone to protect him because pigeons were easy prey for many birds and animals.

Henry leapt into the sky, and Anthony followed a few inches behind. If anyone looked at the pair, they would not see Anthony because his body was so slight compared to Henry's.

The pair flew on, hour after hour, because pigeons also have great stamina. They approached the mountains of Colorado and swung south to avoid the tall peaks. It did not take long before they altered their course to the southwest, but always they were slowly entering higher and higher country. When it was time to stop for the night, Henry spotted a pond in the distance and flew toward it. As he approached, he saw that there were several small buildings and a few trees around the pond.

They landed near the pond and Henry led Anthony to the pond. Henry swam and groomed while Anthony watched. Henry tried to convince Anthony to jump into the water, but Anthony was almost rude in his reply that he was not a goose. Pigeons do not float or swim. He made it clear to Henry that he was purely a land and sky bird. Water was for the ducks and geese.

They had landed on a small, isolated ranch. It was operated by a middle-aged man, his wife, and their 8-year-old daughter. They lived many miles from any doctor, gas station, or convenience store. They produced most of their own food and depended on 100 hens to provide eggs and meat. They used a few eggs to hatch chicks to replace the aging hens, which were then used as food. It was a process that suited everybody, except the hens.

The problem was that many coyotes lived in the area, and their favorite food was chicken. Every night, all year long, the chickens were locked inside their coup at dusk and only allowed out in a fenced-in area again at dawn. This was to protect them from the coyotes and other predators.

Henry heard the chickens cluck as the rancher's wife came to feed them before locking them in at night. Oats and corn were placed inside the hen house to encourage the hens to move inside. Henry and Anthony approached the hen house and saw the chickens going inside. He sensed there was food inside. Henry had never seen a chicken before and found them to be very ugly compared to geese.

They waited for the lady to return to her house before they flew over the fence. They walked to the chicken door and looked inside. Seeing the chickens eating, they stepped inside the hen house and headed toward the feeder. It was a welcome site after their long flight. The food was delicious, but chickens made odd sounds; although, none protested sharing food with the two visitors.

Since he was small, Anthony had trouble pushing his way to the feeder. The chickens pushed him away because they were larger and stronger than he was. They meant no disrespect to Anthony, but they all wanted a place at the trough and the trough was not long enough to accommodate all at once. Henry solved this problem by going to the end of the trough and pushing back, thus opening a small space. He invited Anthony to step up and eat. No three-pound chicken could push a 15-pound goose.

It was now dusk and a little girl appeared to lock the chicken coup door to protect the chickens from predators. She skipped and sang to herself like most happy little girls. She grabbed the door, as she had done a thousand times before, and shut it. However, she forgot to check to see if a smaller chicken door, located inside the fence, had been opened. It had been opened and now remained opened. It was through this door that the chickens passed between the inside and outside of the chicken coup.

After they ate, the chickens found a spot on a roost and crowded together for warmth. They left Anthony and Henry alone on the floor. Henry lifted his wing and Anthony walked in and turned around to face the same direction as Henry, who lowered his wing and they fell asleep.

Before dawn, Henry heard a noise outside. It sounded like an animal running and sniffing. It was a coyote; who went around the fence perimeter, sniffing and tugging at the fence. He sought a weak point where he could enter. After a few moments, and some digging, Henry knew the coyote had gained entry inside the fence. He woke Anthony and directed him to hide inside one of the upper level nests, where the chickens lay their eggs. Henry focused on the small open door knowing this was the only place the coyote could enter. He extended and lowered his neck and stretched his wings as he prepared for combat. Most of the chickens continued to sleep, absolutely helpless and unaware of the danger. They had no defense against the coyote, and the coyote knew it. He expected an easy entrance, a delicious feast, and an easy exit.

Henry was ready. He saw the coyote's head appear through the small doorway. The coyote crunched down and crawled through the door, and then he stopped to view his options. To his astonishment, he heard Henry hissing a warning. The coyote had set his mind on chicken and would not back down. Before the coyote took one step forward, Henry flew towards him, biting the coyote's ear while flapping his wings wildly to keep the coyote off balance. A goose's wings are strong because they are accustomed to carrying the equivalent of a bowling ball hundred's of miles a day, and Henry's wings were stronger than most geese's.

The coyote yelped in pain and surprise. The fight was on. The chickens screamed and bunched up in the back of the hen house. They were filled with fright because they did not recognize any of the horrific sounds in the night's air. The coyote grabbed Henry's chest while Henry grabbed the coyote's tail. The coyote received a mighty blast from a wing and fell back. Henry honked and the coyote howled as they rolled around the floor of the hen house.

Anthony peeked from the nest and saw Henry receiving the worst of it. Unable to stand by and watch, Anthony jumped from the nest and flew towards the coyote's eyes. The coyote flung his head sideways to dislodge Anthony because his hold was very painful to the coyote. Anthony was cast into the wall where his wing hit the sharp edge of a two-by-four stud. He slid to the floor with pain shooting through his wing. All he could do now was watch. Anthony was small and had a broken wing, but he was no coward. Each time the entangled warriors came close to Anthony, he tried to kick or bite the coyote as he passed.

The fight was even, until Henry remembered how Father Goose had ended his fight with a coyote. Henry waited for an opening and then grabbed a sensitive spot, and he squeezed like there was no tomorrow. He felt the coyote release his bite, and then came the yelp that was heard for miles. The fight was over. The coyote tried to find the open door, but he had to drag Henry with him as he scrambled toward the door. He crawled through the door dragging Henry, who had his feet braced stiffly. When the coyote was racing through the door, Henry released his grip. The threat was over. The coyote yelled with every step of his retreat. It was pitiful. Henry was proud, because no one was hurt while he was on guard, just like his father.

Henry went to see if Anthony was hurt. At the same time, the humans' house door opened and voices approached the chicken coup. The door opened, and the rancher's wife looked inside and saw all the chickens bunched on one side. She flashed her light around the floor to determine the extent of the damage. She saw one goose and one wounded pigeon. She continued to look around, and then, startled, she returned to the goose and pigeon. She focused the light on Henry's face. He smiled widely at her. She dropped the light beam to his feet. She saw Henry's white shoe. Her mouth dropped before she could slowly slur "Buuuuutch!?!?"

The rancher had a flashlight and was inspecting the fence. He yelled, "It was the coyote again. How many did he kill this time?"

His wife stuttered, "Buuuutch!?!?!," again and then, regaining control, managed to say, "Butch, come here. You are not going to believe this."

Butch slapped his hand against his leg and muttered something not worth repeating as he walked toward the large door. He expected heavy losses. As he arrived at the door, he saw Henry wearing his white boot and a smile, and Anthony with his wing extended limply at his side, and no hen fatalities. They may not lay eggs for a few days, but they were all alive.

Butch and his wife were puzzled, since it was not an everyday occurrence to see a smiling goose with a white boot accompanied by a pigeon with a broken wing in their chicken coup. Apparently these two gave a serious thrashing to a coyote.

Butch asked his wife, "Do you think that the goose was the one who beat the heck out of the coyote?"

His wife said that geese were good fighters, and she saw no one else in the chicken coup that could have been responsible. Anthony understood this comment and showed his disgust by ruffling his feathers, puffing out his chest and taking two steps forward.

Butch observed, "That coyote could have easily killed 10 or more chickens. We owe these guys." His wife agreed. Her mouth was still ajar.

The wife said, "I doubt if they can fly for awhile. The pigeon may have a broken wing. It sure is bent funny. Perhaps they'll let me attend to their wounds."

Butch responded, "I've never seen a goose or a pigeon sit still while a person doctored its wounds."

The wife retorted, "How many times have you seen a goose and pigeon in a chicken coup? Besides, the goose has a white boot. You don't suppose he made that by himself, do you?

Butch relented and changed the subject, "Have you noticed that the goose isn't nervous around us?"

The wife returned with her animal first aid kit. She talked soothingly as she approached Henry and Anthony. Henry understood and took a few steps toward her. After his friendship with the Cobbler, Henry was confident in his ability to judge human intentions. She cleaned his cuts and placed a healing cream on them. Henry was done. He stepped back and honked gratefully. She continued to talk gently while she looked at Anthony. Anthony looked at Henry, and Henry gave an encouraging honk. Not convinced, but placing faith in Henry's opinion, Anthony took several steps forward. Anthony covered the same distance as Henry, only his steps were much shorter. The rancher's wife carefully looked at his wing. She knew that it was broken and it must be hurting Anthony. She dripped a drop of pain medicine on the cut and hydrogen peroxide to clean it. She carefully set the wing and tied two Popsicle sticks around it as a splint. That was the best she could do.

Before they left, the wife mentioned to Butch that she thought she saw a number on Henry's white foot. They focused the light on it and wrote down a number that might be a telephone number and quietly backed out the door and locked it. They also locked the small chicken door and returned to their house.

They looked at the number and dialed it. They waited as the telephone rang. The Cobbler answered. The rancher's wife explained the strange situation to the Cobbler, who laughed, perhaps for the first time in decades. The Cobbler explained the foot and gave a brief history on Henry. The rancher's wife inquired about the pigeon. The Cobbler knew nothing about a pigeon, but he was certain that any bird with Henry would be as kind and gentle as Henry. He expressed his gratitude for their taking care of Henry and his friend.

They thanked the Cobbler and thought about sleep, but the evening's events were so strange that Butch could not sleep. His wife put water on to boil for a cup of tea. Butch grabbed the whiskey bottle, and they sat at the kitchen table smiling at each other and shaking their heads in disbelief. No one would believe this story.

The next morning, the little girl was told of the miracle. She ran out of the house directly to the chicken coup. She opened the chicken door and filled the feeders with corn and oats. She looked for the miracle, and she smiled and giggled at the same time when she saw Henry, but she did not see Anthony. Her smile froze as she began to look nervously around for Anthony. When Henry stood up to walk to the feeder she saw that little Anthony had been safe and warm under Henry's wing. Her smile returned.

She knew she should not make sudden sounds or movements, so she stood there and watched the miracle unfold. She was elated. She was only eight years old, but wise enough to recognize that few humans would ever see what she was witnessing.

Henry opened a space for Anthony, and they both ate peacefully with the chickens. Their bodies ached from the fight with the coyote, but their hearts were happy. Henry admonished Anthony for not following his orders to stay in the nest. Anthony told Henry that friends lived together and died together. One friend cannot watch from a safe place while another is harmed in any way. It was his duty, as a friend, to join the fracas, even if it meant death. There was no other honorable way. Henry knew this was correct and that Anthony was a true and courageous friend.

chapter

EIGHT

Since Anthony could not fly until his wing healed, they stayed at the farm longer than they had planned. They were in no danger in the chicken coop. Every morning they happily ate the corn and oats provided by the little girl. She always stayed and watched them eat. At dusk, she was careful to close all doors to the chicken coop, so neither her new friends nor the chickens were hurt. Everyone slept peacefully. There were no more attacks on the chickens because the predators knew Henry and Anthony were inside.

Every morning, the doors were opened and feeders filled. Henry and Anthony were in heaven. Their weight increased each day because they ate often and never exercised. Every day Anthony's wing hurt less, and slowly, he became stronger.

After a few weeks, Anthony could use his wings. One day both Henry and Anthony flew out of the chicken yard and again visited the pond. Henry swam and dipped his head into the water while Anthony fluttered his wings to try them out. Then, they returned to the safety of the yard. They decided it was time to depart.

The following morning when the little girl was feeding everyone, Henry approached her and honked tenderly. He looked directly at her, cocked his head, and honked again. Anthony also came closer to the little girl, but he did not come as close as Henry because he did not have the same trust in humans as Henry did.

The little girl sensed something was happening and called for her mother, who appeared at the door still wearing her apron. She dried her hands as she looked at her daughter, who motioned her mother out to the chicken coop. The mother walked to her daughter's side, squatted and put one arm around her daughter's waist. Henry took one step in her direction and repeated his tender honks. The mother looked at Henry, who looked straight into her eyes. After a moment's silence, the mother told her daughter that Henry and Anthony might be leaving. They appeared to be healed. People who work with animals develop a deep level of understanding and can sense what animals are feeling. Butch's wife was one who could.

The daughter's eyes filled with tears. She asked her mother if they could keep Henry and Anthony. She pleaded that they were her favorite pets. But the mother explained that they could not hold them captive. They were not pets. They were wild creatures. It would not be right to imprison them. Henry and Anthony came to them voluntarily and performed a heroic act by defending their hens. They asked for nothing. They should not be asked to give up their freedom for a selfless act.

The daughter objected meekly, but she knew her mother was right. Henry and Anthony were free spirits, and they must be able to wander. The mother explained to her daughter that they had enjoyed Henry and Anthony's presence. The mother told her daughter that the strange pair of birds might decide to return to their ranch in the future.

They both stood and stepped back. The little girl bravely said goodbye as she waved to the pair. Tears filled her eyes. Henry and Anthony turned away and pointed their beaks westward and jumped into the air. Within seconds they disappeared from sight. The mother consoled her daughter as they returned to the house. The daughter sobbed quietly, but she was happy-sad, not sad-sad.

Henry and Anthony were happy to be flying again, though Henry was out-of-shape and Anthony's wing was still sore. Anthony took his place on Henry's left, and mile by mile, they continued westward.

After a few hours, Anthony signaled to Henry that he needed to rest. His wing hurt, so they found a sheltered area and landed. Henry understood, but he also felt conflicted and felt strongly that the Great Goose needed him to continue his flight. Henry thought for a second, and then had an idea. He offered his shoulder blades as a platform for Anthony, who could hang onto Henry's feathers with his claws while Henry's strong wings carried them both.

Henry thought he could fly and carry Anthony since Anthony was not large; however, Anthony was not interested. Anthony bluntly said that it was the most stupid idea that he had ever heard. Pigeons are birds and fly for themselves, not on the back of a goose. The idea was absurd, said Anthony, but Henry explained he felt an urgency to continue. It was the Great Goose's will. Finally, Anthony became quiet, but he was still not convinced. To compromise, Anthony suggested they try the idea now, and if it worked, they could continue tomorrow, but if Henry tired from carrying the extra weight, or if Anthony could not hang on to Henry's feathers, they would land and spend the night. Anthony finally agreed.

In preparation, Henry stretched his wings, and Anthony hopped onto his back. Anthony tried to find a spot between Henry's shoulder blades that seemed balanced. He then carefully pinched his claws together for a grip. Finally, Henry jumped into the sky and started pumping his wings. He almost did not stay in the air, but he adjusted and maintained flight. Anthony was small, but he was extra weight that Henry was not used to carrying.

Henry flew another couple of hours, but he tired. They looked for a spot and found a large pond with some trees. Anthony released his grip from Henry's back as they landed. Anthony did not trust Henry's legs to absorb the shock of them landing together, especially since Henry had only one real leg.

Henry went swimming while Anthony looked around for places where they might eat. Anthony was always hungry, and Henry liked a dip in water to relax before eating.

After a while Henry felt rested. He climbed from the water and looked around for Anthony. It was not like Anthony to go far on his own, because it was dangerous. What if he was attacked by a predator, or if he became lost again. Henry felt a sudden fright for Anthony's safety.

Henry honked loudly to signal Anthony that he was ready to eat. If Anthony was lost, he could fly toward the honks. Anthony suddenly burst over the hill followed by a larger bird. Henry felt an adrenalin rush fearing Anthony was in danger of being attacked by a predatory bird. While Henry was honking, as geese always do before jumping into the air, Henry perceived that Anthony was in no danger. He stopped honking, relaxed his wings and waited on the ground for Anthony's arrival.

Anthony and the other bird landed near Henry. The strange bird was a duck. Anthony looked at Henry and said, "This is Gilbert. I found him in an area full of seeds. The poor guy is alone too. He became detached from his flock during a storm and has not been able to find them."

Gilbert and Henry exchanged honks, quacks, and looks. Anthony suggested they stay together for the night. They would be better protected as a group than as individuals. It was agreed.

They returned to the seeds and ate. Then they found a spot to sleep, but sleep was slow in coming. Gilbert asked where they were flying. Anthony said he was with Henry, because he had lost his own way. Gilbert asked Anthony if he was a homing pigeon. Anthony proudly responded that he was. Gilbert wise-cracked, "And you are lost? You're a homing pigeon, and you are lost?"

Anthony did not like the duck's tone and fired back, "Well, didn't you lose your flock, or am I wrong?"

Gilbert ignored the question, and asked Henry where he was going. Henry said that he was not sure where they were going, but he was sure they would soon arrive. This revelation seemed to interest Gilbert. He said, "So, a homing pigeon, who cannot find his way home, is following a goose, who does not know where he is going, but knows he will soon be there?"

Henry confirmed that Gilbert understood the situation perfectly. Gilbert shook his head in disbelief but wisely remained silent. Anthony was already testy and ready to counter any verbal assault with physical violence, if necessary. He did not want to be insulted.

Henry decided to volunteer more information before Gilbert thought they were crazy. He explained that he was on a mission for the Great Goose. It was He, the Great Goose, who was directing him. As Henry spoke a smile appeared on Gilbert's face.

Gilbert questioned mockingly, "Great Goose?"

Henry continued, "Yes. Geese are often directed, or coached, by the Great Goose. He is the wise one given to us by the Great Creator to help us."

Gilbert echoed, "Great Creator?"

Henry was surprised that Gilbert had not been educated in these matters. He thought that all birds were oriented by their gaggles. He explained, "In the beginning, the World was created by the Great Creator. He created the day and then the night followed by the dusk and dawn. He became lonely and created birds and animals. He was still lonely so He created the humans. The humans required much more of His time than He had planned, so He provided the geese with their Great Goose. The Great Goose was responsible only for the geese and had the wisdom of the ages. Geese learned quickly from the Great Creator and His assistant, the Great Goose, and adapted good behaviors."

Henry continued to explain that not all geese can hear the Great Goose, because their minds are not quiet and receptive. The more receptive a goose is to the Great Goose's counsel, the more likely he will hear and follow it. Geese that follow the counsel of the Great Goose live longer and are happier than those that do not.

Henry asked Gilbert if the Great Creator had also given the ducks a Great Duck. Gilbert thought before responding, "No, not to my knowledge. At least no Great Duck helped me to stay with my flock when I became lost. Who told you there was a Great Goose?"

Henry explained that his Mother and Father Goose told him about the Great Goose, though it was no secret among geese. All geese knew about the Great Goose, but not all can hear his counsel. Some geese do not listen while others ignore it.

Gilbert asked Anthony if there was a Great Pigeon. Anthony said that he had never heard of one, and if there was one, he should have been able to find his way home. He said that the only great pigeon he knew was his mother. She was great, and he missed her very much.

Sleepiness arrived and the talk slowed and finally stopped. Henry raised his wing and Anthony walked in and turned around. Henry dropped his wing, and they slept. They were all tired and felt safe in each other's presence.

The next morning Henry asked Gilbert if he wanted to join their small gaggle. Gilbert saw no harm in that. He enjoyed the company, and it was safer to be in a group than to be alone. Henry offered Gilbert the position on his right. Anthony jumped onto Henry's back, and they all jumped into the air. They flew steadily for several hours before Henry tired. Then, in the distance, they saw a huge flock of large birds, all circling. As they flew closer they recognized the birds as geese.

chapter

NINE

Andy and Leroy were two old friends who had been together for many years. Their partners had recently died. Now, Andy and Leroy were always together. It was as if they did not have individual names. No goose ever asked, "Where's Leroy?" or "Where's Andy?" They always asked "Where're Andy and Leroy?" like they were one goose.

Andy and Leroy were not ready to find new mates. One reason was that young female geese preferred young ganders. No goose wanted an old gander. Andy and Leroy's mating days were gone forever. They missed their life-partners often, but the pain of their absence was lessened with each other's company.

One day they were in a favorite area when a gander arrived, or, more accurately, fell from the sky. He hit the ground in front of them and bounced. Curious, Andy and Leroy walked towards him. They thought he had been shot. They were surprised when he lifted his head, looked at them, and said, "Wow, man!"

The fallen goose tried to collect his thoughts. Andy and Leroy saw the wheels turning in his mind, but they were taking him nowhere. He again tried to focus and when that failed, he repeated, "Wow, man! Those were the most amazing berries I ever tasted." Then he burped and closed his eyes, and his body relaxed. Andy and Leroy's sense of smell was still sharp, and when the foul burp reached their nostrils, they both stepped back.

Andy and Leroy looked at each other. They wondered to what berries he was referring. Andy deduced, "His beak is pointed south so he was flying south when he fell. The berries must be north of here."

Leroy continued Andy's logic, "They mustn't be far because this goose was not capable of flying far."

Andy and Leroy had nothing important to do, and they were always hungry. They decided to look for the berries. They jumped into the air in search of the berry patch. They flew north and within a few minutes they found a place where several geese were flying in circles while others formed a line on the ground. They were eating.

They landed and approached the line. Addressing no one in particular, Andy said, "I heard there were some good berries here." No one answered. In fact, no one noticed them.

Andy looked at Leroy and said, "What do you think? Shall we give it a try?"

Leroy advanced to the red berries on the ground and snapped one up. "Hmmm, these are good, Andy, oh, boy! You'll like them." Andy joined him.

They ate and ate. They moved a little here and there to find the best berries. They ate their fill and moved away from the line. They both felt an unfamiliar strange feeling. They bumped into each other as they walked away from the berries. They were not steady on their feet, but they began to feel strange in other ways also.

Once they distanced themselves from the berries, Andy asked Leroy, "How do you feel, ol' friend?"

Leroy replied, "Those were the best berries I have ever tasted. Why, if I didn't need to take a little nap, I would be out talking with the lady geese. I feel the old magic coming back. I swear Andy, I feel like I'm three years old again."

Andy nodded in agreement as they continued to walk and bump into each other. They found a nice place to sleep and settled to the ground where they continued to lean on each other.

Leroy, always the more talkative of the two said, "Hey, Andy, have you ever thought about spending time somewhere else? I mean far away."

Andy thought a moment then said, "Where else is there to go? This is about the only place we know." They both fell silent and then slept.

The next morning, they were slow to wake. The geese that were eating the berries honked and squawked loudly. Andy shook his head and realized that they he had a headache. They tried to remember what had happened the previous night, but only bits and pieces were recalled.

A goose passed and Andy asked, "Excuse me, friend, but how long has this feast been going?"

The goose looked up and replied, "Oh, I think it's been several days now, but I can't say for sure. I am not good at separating the days." Then, he volunteered, "There have been many flying accidents around here. You guys, being geezers, should be very careful. Several geese have flown into the tree, and some have even had accidents with vehicles on the highway."

Andy was slightly perturbed by this young gander's reference to his and Leroy's age, but asked anyway, "What do you mean by accidents?"

The goose answered, "Some of the berry-eaters play Chicken with the cars and trucks." He paused and shrugged his wings. "The vehicles always win, it seems." He reasoned, "After the geese eat the berries, they do crazy things. Everyone knows the game, Chicken, is intended to help young geese improve their flying skills, but Chicken should never be played with vehicles. That is something only crazy geese do."

He paused a moment and then asked, "Do you know why they call it 'Chicken?'" Without waiting, he answered, "Because that's how smart you have to be to play it." He cackled at his own humor and continued toward the berries. Andy and Leroy only looked at each other.

Andy and Leroy decided to return to eat more berries. As they were eating, a young gander walked up next to them. The gander said nothing. He just ate. Then, he lost his balance and fell into Leroy. "Hey, friend! Are you ok?" Leroy asked.

The young gander looked at Leroy. He seemed to see no one, but he pointed his beak toward the sound and responded, "I'm really fine. I mean...'re-al-ly fine.'" After a slight pause he continued, "Why would you ask, anyway? Is something wrong?" He did not wait for an answer, but returned to eating berries, as did Leroy.

Shortly Andy and Leroy began to feel better, younger, and more energetic. They began to recall their escapades when they were young ganders, and the young lady geese looked at them with interest. They were indeed revitalized and youthful. They noticed that the young gander broke away from the berries and walked with great difficulty. Andy and Leroy stopped eating to watch. They saw the problems he had walking. He extended his wings to help keep him vertical. He looked like a goose walking with training wheels.

The young gander looked ahead toward the tree. He gave the "taking off, all clear, move out of the way" honk and started down the runway. He gained a few feet of altitude and was closing the distance on the tree. Andy said, "He ain't gonna make it!"

Leroy replied, "Nope! Not even close." With that, the goose smacked the tree. He remained stuck to it for a second, and then slid down to the grass. The goose had landed.

For a moment, the fallen goose was immobile; then one wing moved, and then the other wing moved, and then up came the head, and finally, the landing gear descended, and the goose was up. He struggled to return to where

Andy and Leroy stood. He looked through them and asked, "Hey, you guys. How many trees do you see over there?" as he pointed his beak toward the tree.

Leroy responded, "One tree. There is definitely just one tree."

The fallen goose asked, "Then why do I see two trees? I see two trees. I definitely see two trees. I tried to fly between them, but I must have hit one of them. I think I need a nap. I am tired. Those berries sure make me tired." He slowly walked away, placing each foot ahead of the other with a very deliberate motion, his wings extended to steady him.

Andy and Leroy began to find it more interesting to watch the other geese. Many of these geese had difficulties walking. They watched one goose that had eaten all afternoon and now made his way away from the shrubs. He jumped into the air and forgot to extend his wings. He crashed onto the ground with a loud thud. After a moment's pause, he shook himself and jumped again. This time he remembered to open his wings, and he slowly gained altitude. He was wise enough to point himself in a direction away from the tree.

Andy and Leroy looked at each other. Each understood that it might be interesting to follow the goose and see where he went. He seemed to be flying with a purpose. They uttered the required "all clear, goose taking off here" honk and jumped into the sky and followed the goose. He gained altitude and flew toward the interstate highway that paralleled the berries. Andy and Leroy followed at a discrete distance. The goose flew east of the highway. Then, suddenly, he turned back toward the highway. He increased his speed. He focused on something, but Andy and Leroy could not determine what it was. Before they could process what was happening, the goose buried his head into the side of an SUV that did not have time to brake before impact, though it skidded to a stop within seconds.

Andy and Leroy were stunned. They circled a couple of times to fix in their minds what had happened and then returned to the berries. They landed and continued to watch the other geese.

Andy and Leroy found the berries very tasty, but they began to distrust the berries. They made them feel young, but the berries seemed to have a strange effect on the other geese. Andy and Leroy were surprised at how many geese became foolish after eating a few berries.

Toward evening, a very strange thing happened, and Andy and Leroy were the only geese to notice. Three huge and very unusual geese appeared in the sky, made their descent and landed. They saw Andy and Leroy and walked toward them. Andy and Leroy honked greetings to the arriving geese. The lead goose honked, but it was in a strange accent and difficult to understand.

The front goose repeated what he had said. Andy and Leroy looked at each other because they could not understand the strange goose. Finally, Andy said, "You folks ain't from around here, are you?" Andy was a geezer gander, but he was still as sharp as a tack.

The goose spoke slower and louder attempting to be understood, "My name is Nicholas. I'm from Russia."

Interested, Leroy said, "You're from where?"

Nicholas repeated, "I'm from Russia."

Leroy said, "Where the heck is Russia? What the heck is Russia? Why do you talk funny?" Leroy's social skills were limited. He said, "I've been here watching the geese eat berries, so, I know you don't talk funny because you've been eating berries. If you talk funny without eating berries, I can't wait until you've had some berries. Maybe then, we can understand you."

Being a more refined gander than Leroy, Andy replied, "Forgive my partner. Leroy has few manners. You say you're from Russia? Where exactly is Russia?"

Nicholas, speaking slowly replied, "It is the region we come from," and he stepped back to introduce the other two geese accompanying him. Nicholas continued, "This is Natasha, my sister, and the other one is my brother, Dmitry." They both slightly dipped their beaks when introduced.

Andy said, "My name is Andy, and my companion is Leroy." Leroy smiled for Natasha.

Andy continued, "I have never heard of Russia. Is it far?"

Nicholas said, "Yes, it is very far. We have flown for many days. We heard about this place two days ago from a goose that was flying north with a small gaggle. He thought he was flying to a warmer climate by flying north. He did not seem right in the head, but who are we to judge another goose, especially when he is from another region? Geese in different regions do things differently. He was happy enough to be traveling, so we did not tell him that temperatures become colder as he goes north. I am sure that eventually he will figure it out."

Leroy, smiling, still looked at Natasha. Andy, always the practical goose, continued to probe Nicholas. "Why are you here? What do you plan to do? Where are you going?"

Nicholas shrugged and said, "We want to see some of the world before we assume our responsibilities in our gaggle. Our mother and father were not happy, of course. We could not convince them that this was good. They were especially against Natasha coming, but she wanted to come. Eventually, they accepted that we were going to take a few months to visit other places. We will soon return. They will see that we will all be safe. I am in charge. I will not allow anything to happen to them. This I promise Mama and Papa."

Leroy continued to focus his smile on Natasha, but Andy invited everyone to taste the berries. He said, "Join us in eating some berries. I don't know about berries in your region, but these are considered very tasty here."

All five geese moved toward the berries. As they approached, the other geese started to stare. The three Russian guests were very different in appearance from the local geese and their accents were noticeably different. They were also twice as large as a Giant Canada Goose. Their appearance was formidable. Andy and Leroy did not know this, but they were Giant Canada geese and the Russian geese were Tula geese, which habitat a region southeast of Moscow. Nicholas and Dmitry were big guys, weighing almost 25 pounds each. Andy and Leroy were plump, but they only weighed 12 pounds each. Another thing that Andy and Leroy did not know was that Russian geese are known in their region as "fighting geese." They can be aggressive and short-tempered.

Andy and Leroy were good feeders, but the Russian geese were better. A 25-pound goose must eat a substantial amount of berries to maintain its weight, and the Russian geese did not intend to lose weight.

It was not long before Andy and Leroy felt young again. Leroy now embarrassed Natasha by staring at her with a silly smile on his beak. Leroy was in love.

As Nicholas reached his fill of berries, he raised his beak and noticed Leroy's attention directed toward his sister. Nicholas shouted, "Hey, what are you looking at? Don't look at my sister like that or I will squawk you like a bug."

Andy looked at Nicholas and then at Leroy, he did not understand. Leroy did not respond, but Andy did, noticing the protective nature of the brother toward his sister. "What do you mean 'squawk you like a bug'?"

Nicholas frowned and showed frustration at not being understood. He repeated what he had said. Andy and Leroy still did not understand. He tried again and used his wings to demonstrate. Andy said, "Oh, you mean 'squash you like a bug.'"

"Yes, squashed like a bug. That is what I said. Do you not hear well? Why must I say everything two times?"

Meanwhile, Dmitry either did not understand anything that was being said, or he did not care. He understood nothing of international relations. He watched some of the young lady geese eating berries. Suddenly, Dmitry left the official reception for the Russian geese. Within seconds he was a few yards away speaking with a young and very attractive Giant Canada goose. Although he spoke little English, his body language was fluent.

Leroy regained his composure and stole quick glances at Natasha. Nicholas ordered, "You leave my sister alone. You do not talk to her and do not try to visit her unless I am present. If you do not obey me, I will thrice you. Do you understand me?"

They did not. They looked at Nicholas with a blank look, and Nicholas immediately repeated, "I will thrice you."

Andy, who was becoming more familiar with the accent, asked, "Are you trying to say 'thrash you?'"

Again, Nicholas responded, "Yes that is what I said. What is wrong with you geese? Are all geese here so hard of hearing that we must repeat everything thrice?"

Andy and Leroy looked at each other and were afraid to ask any questions. They thought it might be better to leave the big guy alone. He was easily agitated and nervous.

chapter

TEN

Henry, Anthony and Gilbert flew toward the circling geese. Anthony's wing hurt causing him to stay aboard Henry as they descended and made a slow, smooth landing near the tree.

Henry and Gilbert turned and walked toward the small group of geese that stood nearby. Anthony had not yet dismounted. As they approached the group, the group was speechless and stood with their beaks open watching Henry with Anthony still on his back, and Gilbert. Henry was the first to speak. "Hello, I'm Henry. The duck is Gilbert, and the pigeon is Anthony."

Leroy recovered first and said, "Henry, did you know you have a growth on your back?"

At that, Anthony leaped from Henry's back and walked threateningly towards Leroy. There was such determination in Anthony's step that even Nicholas began to smile with respect. Anthony sputtered as he stomped closer and closer to Leroy. Since his steps were small, it took a while. He said, "Why is it that almost every goose I meet is dumber than a duck? No offense, Gilbert. Why, compared to you a chicken is a genius. What do you mean, 'a growth?' Do I look like a growth?"

Henry started to step between them, but before he could, Leroy accepted the challenge. Leroy said, "I'm sorry. You don't look like a growth. You look like a runt, and if you don't know what that is, it's a lack of growth. And you're ugly, too." Anthony was preparing to jump on Leroy's head when Henry intervened.

Henry pleaded for reason by saying, "Gentlemen, let's be nice. Anthony is a homing pigeon, and he is my friend. We have traveled together for many days, and he deserves to be treated with respect."

With that, Anthony returned to Henry's side, where he stood tall and proud. Gilbert inadvisably added, "Homing pigeons can always find their way home, but Anthony is having a few problems in this area."

A smile spread over Leroy's face. Anthony put on his fighting face and started to advance again, but Henry stretched his wing to stop Anthony, who reluctantly retreated.

Anthony said, "Gilbert, why don't you tell the group why you are flying with Henry and me?" Gilbert understood the situation and said no more.

Andy stepped forward and said, "I think you have already met our always witty Leroy." Leroy shot Andy a contemptuous look. Andy continued, "My name is Andy. Leroy and I have been friends for many years. These three geese are from a place called Russia. They have flown far to be with us. Their leader is called Nicholas. His beautiful sister is Natasha," and as he spoke he looked at Nicholas to see if his comment would bring any reprisal, "and the one with a smile is Dmitry."

Henry, Anthony, and Gilbert dipped beaks and honked welcomes. Perhaps not fully understanding what had just transpired, Nicholas asked Henry, "Are you brothers?"

Henry responded, "No, we're friends."

Nicholas continued, "Why are you so different in size? Did you have a different father?"

Henry smiled and explained, "No, we are not related. In fact, we are completely different."

Nicholas failed to fully capture the English and questioned, "But why are you so different in size? Did your mama not treat you the same? How is it that Anthony is such a weak runt and you are so large and strong?"

Anthony understood Nicholas's question, and he started toward Nicholas while saying, "Listen to me, you big, dumb, deformed duck, or whatever you are. You can't talk to me like that. I will rip out your eyeballs."

Henry placed his wing between Anthony and Nicholas and pushed Anthony back.

Henry smiled. He liked Nicholas, because he recognized a strong and good goose. He thought how he might better explain to Nicholas the differences among geese, ducks and pigeons. Henry started by asking, "Nicholas, look at the green grass. Now look at the green shrubs. Now, look at the green tree."

Nicholas obeyed, but did not yet see the point.

Henry said, "Anthony is the grass; Gilbert is the shrub; and I am the tree. We are similar, but very different. Henry illustrated two different trees and explained that Henry was one tree and Nicholas, Natasha, and Dmitry, were the other tree. Nicholas nodded, but he still did not understand.

Andy had been listening, but he had also been thinking and asked Henry, "Why did you carry Anthony on your back? Can't he fly?"

Henry quickly extended his wing and caught Anthony as he started his assault on Andy. Henry replied, "Anthony is an excellent flier." Hearing this, Anthony's chest expanded. Henry was the smartest goose he had ever met. Perhaps that is why they were such great friends. He did not think he could be friends with any bird that was dumb.

Henry continued his story, "Anthony has a wing that is still healing. It was broken in a fight. Since we are friends and want to stay together, and I must continue my journey, I carry Anthony on my back when his wing hurts."

Leroy asked unbelievably, "Anthony was in a fight? What with...a mouse? And the mouse won, right?" Leroy chuckled with satisfaction at his response, but was surprised when Henry clarified, "No, it was with a coyote."

Everyone gasped and looked at Anthony with disbelief. Anthony stood so tall and wide that Henry thought he might explode. Anthony thought that Henry was a true friend, one worth dying for should the occasion arise.

With the introductions made, all misunderstandings removed, and explanations complete, Andy invited everyone to eat berries. They waddled toward the line. No one noticed that Natasha was stealing glances at Henry as they walked. She thought Henry was a very imposing, handsome, and thoughtful goose.

Natasha walked a step or two behind Nicholas, making it difficult for him to know if she showed interest in anyone. When they reached the berries, they ate their fill. Andy and Leroy again began to feel young and energetic. Leroy glanced at Natasha. He was the first to notice that she was looking at Henry. Leroy was jealous and tried to attract Nicholas's attention. He wanted Nicholas to stop her flirting with Henry. Leroy bumped Nicholas and rolled his head toward Natasha. Nicholas already did not like Leroy so he asked Leroy, "You have problem in neck or in head? I think you have problem in head. You want I should fix your problem?" Leroy thought it better to not bother Nicholas any further.

Finally, everyone had eaten. Nicholas, Dmitry, and Natasha did not feel any effect from the berries, but Leroy was in love. He did not know what to do. He felt compelled to act since Natasha was showing an interest in Henry. If Leroy did not act, Natasha would choose Henry, and he would still be alone.

They walked away from the berries toward an area where there was shade and grass. They sat and started poking for grass sprouts. Leroy was desperate. He tried to position himself away from Nicholas and close to Natasha.

This was not easy. He tried to attract her attention, but he could not. Finally, he stood and started clowning. He thought it might catch her attention, He was right. Natasha saw it and smiled. He was performing a funny step he invented during his earlier courting days. Leroy was the only goose able to perform this unusual set of steps, so other geese affectionately referred to it as "Leroy's Walk."

Unfortunately for Leroy, Nicholas also saw it. As Leroy performed for Natasha, he did not see Nicholas coming until he felt several tail feathers pulled from their roots. Leroy screamed from pain. He looked around and saw Nicholas spitting out a beak full of feathers. He also saw Natasha laughing. Leroy was crushed.

chapter

ELEVEN

The friends spent hours resting in the shade. Gilbert heard a noise and searched the horizon for its source. He saw a man and a dog appear at the hill's crest. The man was carrying something in his hands. Gilbert said, "What do you suppose he's doing here?"

Andy and Leroy were more experienced geese. Andy yelled, "That's a shotgun and it is used for killing geese, and the dog chases geese. They are dangerous. We need to leave." With that, they gave the takeoff warning, and they followed Andy out of the area, staying close to the ground as they flew.

The other geese had not noticed the man and his dog as they came closer and closer to the berry-eating geese.

The dog remained at the man's side with his ears held high in expectation. The official hunting season had not opened yet. Unaware, the other geese continued to arrive and leave. Those leaving were slower and less alert than those arriving. Suddenly, the man raised his gun and with three quick pops, three geese fell lifelessly to the ground. The man yelled an order, and the dog retrieved the geese, one at a time, placing them at the man's feet. The man lowered his shotgun and put the geese into a bag. The man and dog returned to his pickup.

Henry said, "Let's follow the man and see where he lives."

Nicholas commanded, "You and I go. The others must stay." None of the geese saw any need to challenge Nicholas's decision, so, only Henry and Nicholas left.

The dirt road made it easy to follow from a distance because of the dust kicked up by the pickup. After a few minutes the truck turned from the road into a farm yard with a house, and stopped. Henry and Nicholas landed on a hilltop and watched the man remove the dead geese by carrying them inside the house. The man returned and placed his dog inside a pen that had high wire walls. He stroked the dog's head and patted him on the back before closing the gate and returning to the house. Henry and Nicholas returned to their camp and explained to the others what they saw.

The next day the same thing happened. They woke and had berries for breakfast, then rested under the shade of trees. The man and his dog appeared a second time. He quickly shot three more geese, the dog retrieved them, and they left.

Andy was the first to speak. He said, "What do we do if the man does this every day? If he returns every day and kills three geese, sooner or later he will kill all of us."

Nicholas quickly replied, "No. I do not leave. I like this place. We make the man leave."

The others were surprised. They never considered this option. They had no clue what Nicholas was talking about. Andy asked the question they all had in their minds, "How do we make the man leave?"

Nicholas answered, "Simple. Dmitry and I will thump him with our wings, and he will go away."

Leroy, silent until now, asked, "What do you mean, 'thump him with your wings?'"

Nicholas explained, "Once, back in Russia, I was going in for a landing on a pond. There were some trees and a sidewalk winding among them. A man was walking on the sidewalk and appeared from behind a tree. He didn't see me and I didn't see him. I hit him in the neck. He fell and didn't move for several minutes. Dmitry and I thought that being able to knock a man down could be useful, so we practiced our skills. Eventually, when people came to our pond and bothered us, we thumped them, and they stopped bothering us."

Nicholas continued, "When the man comes, he comes to hunt. He will not expect any attack by us. He comes and looks at the geese before he shoots them. We will wait for him to come tomorrow. When we see him leave his truck Dmitry and I will fly high and behind him. As he reaches the top of the hill, Dmitry and I will fly close to each other so that my wing touches Dmitry's body and Dmitry's wing touches my body. We do not flap wings. We glide by dropping our heads and falling toward the man. We hit him behind the neck. He will fall down, and then he will go home and never return."

Leroy's beak was open in awe. He asked, "You can do that?"

Nicholas answered, "Sure, Dmitry and I did that many times as young ganders. Humans do not like it. They go away."

The next day was a repeat of the two previous days. They ate. They rested. The man and his dog returned. As soon as they left the truck, Nicholas and Dmitry took to flight. As the man and his dog calmly walked up the hill, unaware of the plan already put into action. Nicholas and Dmitry gained altitude and positioned themselves behind the hunter. When the man and his dog reached the top of the hill, Nicholas and Dmitry increased their speed by losing altitude. Only inches separated their bodies. Each goose's wing overlapped the other goose's body. They hit the man in the back of the neck knocking him from his feet and flipping him before hitting the ground. In the process he jammed his finger into the trigger exploding the shotgun. The man yelled loudly in pain and looked at his boot where he saw blood pouring out.

The man had no idea what had happened. He did not see the geese hit him and did not see them fly away after hitting him. He looked at his foot and knew that he had shot himself. He slowly and painfully limped back to his truck with his dog by his side.

He knew he could not treat his foot himself. It was too badly damaged. It had to be examined by a doctor. He started toward the city to visit his doctor. As he drove, he tried to create a believable story about cleaning his gun and having it fire accidentally. For an experienced hunter, that would be an embarrassing story, but he could think of no better alternative.

Nicholas and Dmitry returned to their friends, who warmly received them.

That night they had a berry snack before retiring to their sleeping area. They were all happy and relaxed. As often happens when friends are happy and under the stars, they started telling stories. Andy told a story about going to the beach and watching people glide on the surface of the water. He described how they swam into the ocean with a huge board and then a wave came and they stood on the board and the waves carried them to the beach. He thought it looked like fun, like flying on the water.

Leroy, not to be outdone by anyone, told of flying high into the mountains and watching humans slide down the snow-covered mountain on sticks attached to their feet. They reached great speeds. Henry wondered how that feeling compared to his flying high into the sky and then diving towards earth.

Henry let Anthony tell the story of the coyote attack. Anthony was good at telling stories. He was very dramatic and he acted the story as much as he told it. Everyone was silent as he spoke. They gasped at the moments when the struggle between Henry and the coyote was in doubt. They cheered when Anthony entered the fight and helped bring it to a quick end. Anthony loved Henry for allowing him to tell the story. Henry agreed to every detail lending credence to Anthony's incredible tale.

Henry relived his adventures while he lived at the University. He told of the challenge with his gaggle-mates and how he won it. The listeners were respectfully silent and gasped at his flying expertise. He continued with the story about the student throwing an acorn, and how he flew at him. Everyone laughed at this. Natasha smiled. She thought that was a gentleman's reaction to defend a young lady. Finally, Henry ended his tales by explaining how he had lost his foot. He described leaving Mother and Father Goose to follow the wishes of the Great Goose. Everyone was very quiet. Leroy thought he saw tears in Natasha's eyes and was jealous.

Andy had to ask Henry, "But if you lost your right foot, what is that white thing?" Henry told the story about the Cobbler, and again, everyone was silent and tears flowed from Natasha's eyes.

Nicholas asked, "Who are Mother Goose, Father Goose, and the Great Goose?"

Henry smiled and answered, "Mother Goose is my mother. Father Goose is my father. And the Great Goose is the Creator of all geese, who guides us in everything we do."

Leroy said, "Great Goose my behind! I am a goose and no one has ever guided me."

Henry said, "Not all geese can hear him. To hear him, a goose must think good thoughts and maintain a clean and pure mind. He guides us through difficult moments. He asks me to do things for him. That is why I am here."

Dmitry broke his silence and asked, "What does this Great Goose want from you here?"

Henry replied, "I don't always know where he wants me to go. I don't know what he wants me to do when I arrive. He guides my heart and I must follow my heart. I can only believe that I have gone where He wants me to go and done what He wants me to do, but I am never certain."

Dmitry replied, "That sounds difficult. I am glad that your Great Goose does not speak my language. I do not think I would like what he tells me."

Anthony was inspired by these stories and so he began a more personal story. He remembered that when he was a young pigeon, his mother and father taught him how to find his way home. His mother told him that whenever he felt lost he should think about her and she would appear and guide him to his destination. He always believed this but when he became disoriented from the storm, it did not work. He tried to focus on her, but either he was not able to concentrate, or she was not able to help. He could not find his way home anymore. He felt so ashamed and he was worried about his mother. Perhaps, she was in trouble and could not help him.

After Anthony finished his story everyone was silent. They did not know what to say. Finally, Andy broke the silence and said, "But Anthony, do you think you couldn't find your way home because, in your mind, you didn't like it there? Is it possible that your home is here with us? If so, then you did find your way home, and you didn't need the special help from your mother. What you've done, my friend Anthony, is far more difficult than going from one place to another place. You've gone from a place where you didn't want to be and have found a place you only envisioned in your dreams. You, Mr. Anthony, are among friends. Although you are a pigeon, always feisty, and sometimes unreasonable, you have become our friend." The gaggle nodded in agreement. However, one or two were nearly asleep.

Andy felt inspired and continued, "We are a special gaggle." It was obvious to all who were not asleep that Andy felt the effects of excessive berry consumption, but he was happy and enjoyed his place in the gaggle. He continued, "Think of it. We have three Canada geese—two old and one young—a pigeon, a duck, and three Russian geese. We are a gaggle of special geese. Separately, we're weak, but together we're strong. We're an international gaggle.

Most of the group was sleepy, or already asleep, but among those not sleepy were Leroy and Nicholas. They remained a few feet away from the rest. Leroy whispered, "I don't want to sleep. Can you think of anything we can do?"

Nicholas replied, "No."

Leroy thought. The wheels of his mind were turning and when this happened no one could predict where they would stop, but finally, they did. Leroy asked Nicholas, "Do you remember the way to that hunter's house?"

Nicholas responded testily, "Of course, do you think I am stupid?"

Leroy knew enough not to answer that question. Instead, he asked, "Would you like to do a fly-by to see what is happening at the hunter's house?"

For the lack of anything better to do, Nicholas answered, "Sure."

They took off as silently as possible, and Nicholas led them to the house. The lights in the house were off and the hunter was asleep. They saw the dog sleeping in its little house. They landed nearby and walked upwind toward the doghouse. They reached the wall of the doghouse and looked at each other, then started to pound their beaks against the dog house. The dog jumped from its sleep and hit its head on the door frame. He ran out and jumped against the fence with his paws and started barking. Leroy and Nicholas flew a few feet and hid behind the garage. A light came on inside the house, and the hunter limped outside and looked around. He saw nothing and commanded his dog to be quiet. The hunter was in a foul mood.

The dog quieted down and reentered its house. The hunter did likewise. Leroy and Nicholas waited. The light disappeared, and the man and dog slept again. Andy and Nicholas returned to the doghouse and repeated the pounding. The dog again jumped up and hit his head and started barking. The lights appeared in the house and seconds later the man opened the door and yelled at the dog.

Andy and Nicholas did this again and again, until the sun began to rise. They thought it best to keep their identity a secret and, before the night completely disappeared, they returned home to camp. They flew in as everyone else prepared for the berry line. Everyone was surprised to see Leroy and Nicholas together as they did not like each other much, but they each displayed a huge and mysterious smile and was ready to sleep. They walked to the trunk of the tree and quickly were asleep. They continued to smile as they slept.

chapter

TWELVE

Sandy was a young college graduate and only recently found her dream job in California working with the Department of Transportation (DOT). She liked working with numbers and found satisfaction studying accident rates. One day she saw numbers that appeared to be incorrect. The data suggested a surge in one-vehicle traffic accidents along a short stretch of interstate where the roads were excellent. There were no sharp curves, and weather seldom influenced driving conditions. The historical accident rate was low; but recently, it had increased dramatically, and this anomaly caught her interest.

Sandy monitored the accident rate for a few more days and noticed that the numbers continued to rise. She indecisively bit her lower lip before grabbing the phone and calling the Highway Patrol. She explained that she wanted the names and phone numbers of the accident victims. They told her they could supply her with the information from the three most recent accidents. Before she could hang up the phone, the Highway Patrol added, as an after thought, that geese were involved in two of the accidents, but not the third. This was surprising and puzzling. She had never heard of geese being involved in vehicle accidents.

She hesitated to gather courage and dialed the first number. A deep, scratchy voice answered. His voice was cautious and slurred. After she explained what she wanted, there was a long pause. The driver took a deep breath and started to tell the story.

He said, "I was driving along, doing the speed limit. I've driven this road twice a week for 25 years, and I ain't ever seen nothin' like it." She detected a note of amazement, or was it fear, in the driver's voice. He started to relive the experience.

He continued, "I had my eyes on the horizon, as always. With these rigs you have to always be aware of the vehicles in front. These rigs don't stop on a dime. And, suddenly, it caught my eye. It appeared to drop from the sky and headed right for the truck. I couldn't believe it at first. That bird was flying straight at me. I swear he saw a big red target on my nose. It was like he locked onto my nose and was going to hit it. Just before impact, I swear he had the most determined look on his face that I have ever seen on a bird. He was determined and angry. He looked very angry. Why would a bird be angry, anyway? He locked on and nothing was going to stop him. That's when I tried to miss him, but a rig like that doesn't stop on a dime, and it doesn't turn on a dime either."

He paused a moment and took a deep breath before continuing, "After my rig stopped, I got out and saw that the bird was a goose. I told my boss the story, but he didn't believe me. It doesn't look like I'll get my rig back. They think I was either drinking or cracking up from driving the same route so long. That damn goose may have cost me my job. If it hadn't slammed into my windshield before my rig rolled, I'd hunt him down and have him stuffed and mounted on my wall."

Sandy was surprised. This was not what she expected. Her interest increased. She made the second call. A woman answered. Sandy explained what she wanted. The woman was the driver of the SUV and seemed anxious to tell her story. She explained that she had been taking her son's soccer team to a game. She had been driving the speed limit when her vision caught something on the left. She turned and saw something flying low. It dropped altitude quickly and increased in speed. It was a goose. She realized it was on course to collide with her car if it didn't change its path.

It flew toward the SUV with purpose. She said, "It seemed to be smiling. Maybe it wasn't smiling, but why would it have his beak open? Can geese fly with their beaks open? When it was evident that we were going to collide, I panicked. I hit the brakes and turned the steering wheel to the right. We slid a long distance before we stopped. Thank God all the kids had their seat belts on!" As an after-thought, she added, "The goose didn't survive. He hit the side of the car. You can still see the imprint of its beak." She paused again, as if visualizing. "I've never seen a beak imprint on a car before. That beak must have been terribly strong. What could possibly make it so strong?" Sandy did not know if the lady was speaking to her or to herself.

The lady continued, "We asked the repair shop to cut out that piece and give it to us. I think it would look nice over the sofa. We want to frame it for our living room. No one would believe us if we couldn't prove it." When she finished, she simply stopped. Sandy imagined her smiling, satisfied that she had told an interesting and unusual story.

Sandy was certain she was onto something. She underlined the name and phone number of the driver of the third accident victim and dialed his number. He was also a truck driver. When he answered and she explained her purpose, he fell into an uneasy silence. After a pause, he said that he was driving along and rolled down his window for fresh air when he felt something come through the window and hit his face. In order to swat it with his left hand, he shifted his grip on the steering wheel to his right hand. Then he saw something in his right field of vision moving away from the truck. He bent his head and looked up to see what it was. That is when he lost control of the vehicle, and it turned over before sliding to a stop in the grassy area between the interstate lanes. She prompted him for more details, but he had said all he was going to say.

She decided to go to her boss with her information. She feared that she might be reprimanded for starting this investigation without permission, but her boss seemed appreciative. Her boss decided that immediate action was needed, since some of these accidents were serious and were continuing to occur. There had been no fatalities yet, but the continuous incidents concerned her boss.

Sandy's supervisor had a dozen signs prepared and placed every few miles on both sides of the interstate along the stretch of interstate where the accidents were occurring. The signs read: "Beware Low Flying Geese!" They wanted to place an outline of a goose diving like a screaming eagle on the sign, but they could not agree whether they should make the goose look like it was smiling or angry. They finally decided that it should be a goose with neither a smile, nor a serious look. Otherwise, people might not take the signs seriously.

They instructed the Highway Patrol to notify them immediately the next time an accident occurred that involved geese. Sandy's supervisor talked to the Chief of Patrolmen. They agreed that this information should be given to patrolmen who worked that stretch of the highway.

It did not take long to receive the call. A goose had just been a victim in an accident with an eighteen-wheeler again. As they hurried to the accident scene, they called ahead and told the officers not to touch the goose. They wanted to do an autopsy and needed an uncontaminated corpse.

They arrived, introduced themselves with their identification badges and were escorted to the victim's body. They brought a small garbage bag to use as a body bag. They scraped the goose from the side of the truck as gently as possibly and tried to pour as much of the corpse into their make-shift body bag as possible. Then they raced to the morgue to have the corpse examined.

The doctor at the morgue was incredulous when they produced the bag and asked for a post-mortem. The doctor's face rarely smiled because he was used to seeing all the unexpected outcomes that life can produce, but his face now bent toward a smile. As he reached to take the bag from the lady's hand, he asked, "What did you call this, and what do you want me to do what with it?" The lady repeated her request for a cause of death. His smile broadened. He was beginning to enjoy his day.

They explained to him the importance of the results, and the doctor regained his serious face and placed the goose on the examining table. He asked the ladies to wait outside, so he could do his work. He did not expect it to take long, since there was not much to examine. Once he was sure they were in the waiting room, he lit a cigarette and decided to relax. His week was busy and, by the nature of his work, a sad one, though things were improving now.

As he leaned down to examine the body, the goose caught on fire with a whoosh sound. The doctor jumped back and threw his cigarette down and squashed it with his foot. He quickly felt his face and hair to determine if they were on fire. They were not. He went to the wall and grabbed a fire extinguisher. The fire was quickly doused. The doctor looked anxiously at the waiting room door. It did not open, so they apparently did not see the spectacle.

The flame had been blue. The doctor, on a hunch, tested the goose's blood alcohol and found it to be very high. It was much higher than the legal limit for drivers. The goose was dead drunk when he hit the truck, beak first.

He removed his plastic gloves as he entered the waiting room. The ladies jumped up and looked at him with eager eyes. The boss blurted, "Well, what was the cause of death?"

The doctor could not resist. He said, "Since every bone in his body was broken, I would say it was from coming to a very quick stop."

The boss was unimpressed and asked, "You know what I mean! Did you find anything?"

The doctor said "Yes. When your goose hit the truck, it was as drunk as a skunk." The doctor was pleased with himself. Humor and verbal reports on "cause of death" were seldom combined. As an after thought, he continued, "Actually, he was drunk as a skunk before impact, too." He smiled inwardly because he had learned not to show emotions.

The ladies were not happy as they returned to their office. What kind of crazy person supplied liquor to a goose? This was a federal offense. Serious traffic accidents were involved and fatalities could occur. They had to act. This person must be found and stopped.

They contacted the Highway Patrol with their results. The chief officer sent his best investigator to the stretch of interstate with orders to find the drunken geese, track them to their place of intoxication, and arrest the people responsible for illegally supplying the geese with alcohol.

It did not take long for the investigator to gather his gadgets and arrive at the stretch of highway where the accidents occurred. Almost immediately he saw a gaggle of geese overhead. Instead of flying in the typical v-pattern, they varied between a u-pattern and a w-pattern. While he tracked them, he zigzagged a few miles. It was not easy. He drove with his head out the car window trying to keep sight of the geese while keeping the car on the road.

Finally, when the geese dropped over a hill and disappeared, he hurried to park his patrol car. He grabbed his binoculars, notepad, camera, and tape recorder and quietly closed the car door so not to alert the suspects. He crossed the road and the ditch then climbed over a fence. He ran slowly up the hill while trying to keep his jigging equipment from announcing his approach.

At the summit, he saw large numbers of geese landing and taking off. He dropped to his knees and carefully laid out his equipment. He lay on his stomach to observe the spectacle. He had never seen so many geese. If it were hunting season, he could quickly bag his limit. He tried to remember if he still had his shotgun in the back of the patrol car, but he refocused on the task at hand.

There was a long line of geese eating. The noise was deafening. Wings flapped and tempers flared as some of the geese nipped each other with their beaks to improve their place in the line.

The investigator took pictures, notes, and recorded the sounds. He saw geese that glided in for a landing, but when their feet hit the dirt, they tumbled head over tail.

After a couple of turnovers, they stood slowly, shook their head a couple times, and flapped their wings.

There was a large tree nearby. The investigator concentrated on that region. A goose walking away from the line caught his attention. He walked slowly, yet purposeful, towards the take-off area. He stopped, shook his head and stretched his wings such that their tips were touching the ground. He looked like a goose with training wheels. He gazed forward intently before jumping into the sky and slowly gained altitude. Before he gained enough altitude, he hit the tree. He rolled down the tree trunk and lay motionless on a carpet of grass. Slowly, he stood, shook his head and body, and walked back to the buffet line with his training wheels extended.

The investigator returned to his vehicle. He felt confident that he had all the evidence he needed. He called the chief officer, who called Sandy's supervisor, who called Sandy. They all rushed to the scene.

When they arrived where the geese were lined up eating something on the ground, Sandy and her supervisor walked to the buffet line and only saw short bushes. The geese were reluctant to open a path for them, but they did. The geese did not like being interrupted while eating at the berry buffet.

Sandy and her boss discovered that the plants were shrubs, which had been planted along the interstate a few months ago by the DOT for landscaping purposes. Several miles had been planted along both sides of the interstate. For reasons unknown, the bushes in this area matured quicker than the rest. They produced a berry, which matured and fell to the ground. The berries accumulated and formed a soggy, juicy substance, which the geese ate. Sandy's supervisor scooped a bit of the substance into a bag, and they left.

She returned to the morgue and found the same doctor working. She knocked on the window. When he turned and saw her, he smiled. This irritated her.

He wondered what she had in a bag this time. He dropped his tools, removed his plastic gloves, and met her half-way in the hall. When he saw the plastic bag, his smile widened. The supervisor handed him the bag and asked him to analyze it for her. He unzipped it, held it to his nose and sniffed. He had a very talented nose. He dipped one finger in it and, to the supervisor's surprise, tasted it. His smile continued to irritate her. He identified it as some type a wine.

The supervisor was astonished. DOT had spent a huge sum only a few months ago to plant these shrubs for interstate beautification. They were environmentally friendly, soothing to drivers, and appropriate to the climate. The state environmentalists checked dozens of factors before approving this shrub for this region, but no one thought to study their wine-producing qualities or to cross-check this with the palates of geese.

As is necessary in such situations, the supervisor reported to her boss, who reported to their boss, who reported to another boss. Within three weeks they were promised heavy machinery that would remove the many miles of wine-producing shrubs.

chapter

THIRTEEN

After hearing the story about people skiing down the mountain on snow, Henry often thought about how it would feel. He wondered if it was like flying high into the sky and then diving towards earth. He loved doing that and then pulling out of the dive at the last moment. The speed and the strain on his wings and the pull on his body excited him.

Henry decided he wanted to visit the mountains and race down the slopes on the snow. Anthony did not like change and preferred to stay at the berry patch; however, with some effort, Henry convinced Anthony to accompany him.

The next day he and Anthony pointed their beaks towards the mountains and jumped into the air. It did not take long before Anthony's wing hurt him and he started to fall behind Henry. Henry knew that Anthony suffered pain when he flew and that he would never admit that his wing was hurting, so Henry suggested that they land and rest for a few minutes. Once on the ground, Anthony accepted Henry's invitation to continue their flight with Anthony riding on Henry's back. Anthony jumped onto Henry's back and carefully grabbed onto Henry's feathers, and they continued their flight.

As they gained altitude the scenery gradually changed. It went from flat lands to gentle hills to steep hills and then the mountains surged from the ground. The trees changed from a few scattered trees to forests of large and thick trees and the temperature steadily dropped.

On and on they flew. It was good to fly together again, just the two friends. Though they had met only a short while ago, neither could imagine life without the other. Henry became a stronger flier from carrying Anthony and Anthony became more outgoing and confident. With Henry by his side, Anthony was sure of himself but he still was not an adventurous bird. He preferred safety to adventure and where he was to where he could be. Henry, on the other hand, always liked to see where the wind went after it passed by his feathers, and where it stopped to turn around before returning to where it started.

They were already high into the mountains when they spotted a small lake and decided to land for the night. Henry was tired. It was difficult flying in high altitudes, especially carrying a passenger. Anthony agreed. Impatient, he dropped from Henry's back and they descended side-by-side to the lake.

Henry was anxious to test the water. He tried to convince Anthony to jump onto his back so that he too could enjoy the swim. Anthony thought this was the most ridiculous suggestion he had ever heard. To Anthony, this was an unnecessary risk and there was no reason for it. Why would a pigeon want to subject himself to water? Water was to drink, not for swimming. He did not understand Henry's fascination with water.

Henry waded into the water and paddled off. He paddled and then drifted, and then he paddled some more. He cherished floating on the water. It relaxed him and allowed him to think more about the Great Goose. He dipped his head under the water and brought it quickly out while shaking his head sideways, making water fly from his head in all directions. He did this again and again while wondering when the Great Goose would reveal his plan. He was not complaining. He was having a very good time. He could not imagine what it would have been like to have stayed at the university campus all this time. It had always been pleasant and safe there, but he truly enjoyed the oddities and excitement that life offered him while he was following the Great Goose and attending to his wishes; whatever they were.

Later, he drifted towards Anthony and waded out of the water. He lifted his wings and flapped them as geese do when they leave the water. It was not required, but it made him feel better, dried his wings and encouraged unruly feathers to return to their places.

Anthony had not explored the area while Henry was in the water because he thought about the creatures out there that would like to eat him. He felt safe when Henry was near him. Henry was a fierce creature while defending a friend; and Anthony admired him.

They were both hungry, but they were unfamiliar with the forests and did not know where to go to find food. Henry suggested they do some low level flying, which would require going between the trees and under the branches. Anthony was not excited about this. He still visualized a monster appearing from behind a tree and eating him; but Henry seemed confident, so they departed.

As usual, Henry led with Anthony on his left wing. Henry flew towards a tree and then rotated ninety degrees to miss it. He repeated the process but in the opposite direction to avoid the next tree. Henry flew slowly so Anthony could keep pace, but Anthony was becoming irritated because he saw no reason for darting among the trees. The proper way to fly was to take the shortest distance between two points.

They finally located a berry patch; however, Henry was suspicious that the berries might make them crazy, like the berries they had found at the other berry patch. Anthony was hungry and did not care if they were like the other berries. He liked them and started eating. After a short hesitation, Henry joined. They ate their fill of the berries; they were delicious, but not nearly as tasty as those in the lowlands.

After eating, they found a spot that offered protection against the elements and from predators. They quickly settled in for the night. They were both tired and sleep quickly overtook them. Anthony awoke many times during the night due to strange sounds. Henry seemed not to hear them. Anthony took comfort from this because Henry had never been caught asleep by a predator yet.

The next morning they woke rested and jumped into the air almost immediately. It would not be long before they saw the snow.

The snow appeared beneath them, first a spot here and there, then more and more. Finally, the ground was covered. The temperature continued to decrease. They flew higher and higher. They saw a band of snow stretching up the mountain, and they flew towards it. As they approached they saw a few large houses and an area without trees that continued to the top of the mountain.

Henry and Anthony did not know this, but they were approaching a ski resort. They flew part way up the ski slope and then settled to the ground to watch as people skied down the slope. Anthony was annoyed because this all looked very un-bird-like and very unnatural. Henry unwittingly opened his beak and smiled as he watched the people speed past at enviable speeds. He saw them as they jumped back and forth changing directions, and the snow flew out. Henry knew that this was fun and that he had to do it.

He told Anthony to follow him and before he could protest, Henry flew up the mountain. He remained within the trees. In unfamiliar places, Henry did not like to allow people to see him. He felt safer. They stopped higher on the mountain. Anthony issued his strongest protest yet, but he knew that Henry had already made his decision to do it. Anthony told Henry that he would find a tree branch and try to stay alive while Henry did whatever foolish thing was rattling around in his tiny goose-head, and he flew off to find a safe branch.

Henry found a small boulder at the tree line and hid behind it. He watched how the skiers passed. He noticed their skis, and looked at his web foot and artificial foot, and then back at the skis. Then, he noticed a young man on a snowboard. There was only one board, and it was wider than the two skis.

He watched for a long time before deciding. He would wait until a snowboarder passed. He would fly out and land on the snow board behind the person, and hitch a ride down the slope. It seemed a reasonable plan to Henry, but Henry either did not understand that when you live on the edge, sometimes you fall off, or perhaps he did not care.

A snowboarder came into view. Henry's body tensed in suspense and he shifted his weight from one foot to the other in anticipation. The snowboarder approached and Henry was ready to follow him. He was visualizing the ride down the mountain. The snowboarder passed and Henry jumped into action and flew after him. It was hard to catch him because he was moving fast. Henry used his wings to guide his feet onto the board, and then he tucked them in as he lowered his feet onto the snow board. As Henry felt his body responding to the movement of the snowboard; he began to smile but the man quickly shifted his weight and changed directions. Henry did not. He was jettisoned from the snowboard and rolled many times before he could steady himself with his wings. He recovered his balance and flew into the trees before he was seen. He did not want anyone to know he was there. Henry shook his head and then his body and wings. After catching his breath, he flew up the slope and waited behind the same boulder. He had to find a way to keep himself on the board as the rider shifted directions. As another snowboarder passed, he noticed that they all wore loose clothing. Perhaps he could use his beak to hold onto the snowboarder, and thus, to the snowboard.

The next snowboarder appeared in the distance and sped down the hill and closer to Henry. Henry tensed and mentally viewed what he had to do. The snowboarder passed and Henry launched himself into the air and pursued him. He used his wings to adjust his velocity so he could settle onto the board behind the snowboarder. When he made it, he used his beak to pinch the clothes. He tried to bring his wings close to his body, but he felt he would lose his balance. His first pinch provided little leverage and no balance. He knew he needed more, so he loosened his grip and tried again. This time he took too large of a bite because he felt something soft. The snowboarder felt a pinch and turned around only to see a goose on his snowboard.

When the snowboarder saw Henry latched onto his pants, he threw his arms out, yelled at the top of his lungs, and fell back from the board. Henry, also now frightened, tried to smile at the snowboarder but the snowboarder did not see because his arms were circling widely as he was falling. Nervous, Henry flew to the safety of the trees. The snowboarder continued down the mountain, sliding on his back and yelling loudly as he went.

Henry found Anthony, who was quick to tell him, "I told you so." Henry simply commanded, "Let's go up the mountain a little farther." Henry was focused. Farther up the mountain Anthony took a position on a tree branch. Luckily for him no one noticed a pigeon because pigeons were everywhere; hence, never out of place. Henry was not as lucky. Anyone who saw a goose at a ski lodge would notice. Henry wanted to be invisible.

Henry found a hiding place and sat to watch the people descending the mountain. He envied them. As Henry and Anthony sat and watched from their places; neither realized that a huge grizzly bear was watching Henry. The bear saw Henry and found him interesting. Perhaps the bear intended to eat Henry, or possibly he was only curious. He took a few steps towards Henry before stopping to sniff the air cautiously.

Henry waited for another snowboarder, unaware that the grizzly was slowly approaching. Henry and Anthony were completely engrossed in the drama unfolding on the ski slope. When the bear was within striking distance, Henry, still unaware, threw himself after a passing snowboarder. The bear, surprised at Henry's sudden move, ran after him. When the grizzly reached the center of the clearing, he realized that he could not catch Henry. He stood to his full height and watched as Henry disappeared down the slope.

At this precise moment, two things happened. First, Anthony saw that Henry was in danger, and threw himself towards the standing grizzly's shoulder blades. He hit the bear exactly at that spot and dug in his claws. He wanted to cause as much pain to the bear as possible so that he would forget about Henry. The bear felt nothing.

The second thing was that a skier was flying down the slope, hit a small bump on the slope, and became airborne. He flew directly towards the bear's back. The skier gasped as he closed the distance between himself and the bear. He thought "Ah, you've got to be kidding!" And then he crashed into the bear's back causing him to lose his balance and fall forward onto the snow. When the bear's body hit the snow, his feet found no grip and slid outwards in all directions. As he slid down the mountain his body gained momentum.

Anthony still clutched the bear's back. He had knocked the bear over and now was riding him down the mountain. Meanwhile, Henry flew towards the snowboarder, but he hit the snowboarder wrong and fell immediately from the board. He glided on his stomach towards the bottom. Henry did not care that he fell. The experience was exhilarating. He almost shouted his happiness to the world as he sped downhill on his bottom.

The snowboarder had felt something hit his board. As fate would have it, it was the same snowboarder that Henry had bit earlier. He looked back and saw Henry sliding on his bottom down the slope behind him. He cursed, lost his balance, and fell again. Now, he also was sliding down the slope on his back.

As the snowboarder and Henry continued downhill, so did the bear, the skier and Anthony. The bear was much larger than Henry or the snowboarder or the skier, and he was accelerating faster and was closing the gap between himself, Henry and the others.

At the bottom, the mountain flattened just before reaching the lodge. At the edge of the clearing, near the lodge, there was a high snowdrift that curved into the air, carved by the winds circling the lodge. A cleaning lady was inside the lodge busily performing her duties. The snowboarder slid toward the house, head first, and hit the snowdrift at high speed. The speed was enough to stand him up as he hit the snowdrift, and then he fell back onto the snow. His snowboard hit the lodge making a loud racket. The cleaning lady looked outside to see what caused the noise and saw the man lying on his back. Henry hit the same snowdrift beak first and, being so light, he was jettisoned skyward and landed gently on the roof. He honked with excitement. He had never had a thrill like that. He was ecstatic. The woman looked at the man on his back, and then at Henry. She was taken by surprise and could not speak. Henry was doing the "Leroy Walk."

The cleaning lady heard another noise coming from the mountain. She looked towards the rise of the mountain and saw the large grizzly bear sliding head first towards her. She did not see Anthony on his back, nor did she hear Anthony yelling. The cleaning lady reached to help the snowboarder up. She was watching the bear as she tried to help the snowboarder, but her hand found nothing where the snowboarded had been. She took her eyes from the bear and looked down. The snowboarder was gone. She looked behind her and saw the door close to the lodge. She quickly followed.

The bear hit the snowdrift and, like the snowboarder, his head was lifted upright, and the momentum caused him to fall over backwards. At the last moment,

Anthony jumped off and flew to meet Henry, who was still jumping around on the roof. The bear lay still on its back with his four feet straight up. The cleaning lady and the snowboarder peeked through the window from the lodge. They did not move. The bear did not move. Henry and Anthony were dancing wildly on the roof.

After a few seconds, the bear growled, shook his head, and rolled to one side. The cleaning lady and the snowboarder stepped back from the window. The bear growled again and shook his head and then all his body. It appeared that he was in pain and trying to push everything that had been dislocated by his fall back into place. He took one step, and then another. Very slowly he headed towards the woods. He was growling as he disappeared into the woods. Then, the skier hit the drift. He was flipped onto his back. He stood up, threw his goggles into the snow drift and cursed as he kicked at the snow before heading into the lodge.

When Henry and Anthony stopped dancing on the roof, Henry tried to tell Anthony what a thrill it was, and Anthony tried to tell Henry what a thrill it was. Anthony finally got Henry's attention and told him how he had saved Henry from the bear and what would have been a painful and sorry end.

Anthony stopped and waited for Henry to thank him. Henry had not heard anything Anthony was saying because, in his mind, he still was sliding down the mountain on the snow. He stood there with a silly, happy grin on his face. Anthony was disappointed. He never expected gratitude for saving Henry's life, but he thought Henry would be more grateful.

chapter

FOURTEEN

The trip back seemed much shorter than the distance to the snowy mountain. They landed by the tree and looked for their friends. Henry had had a wonderful time and was visibly content, but Anthony was a changed pigeon. He now exuded confidence and was ready to attack the world. He felt that, if he could subdue a grizzly bear, and ride him down the mountain, he could do anything. He was empowered.

Henry and Anthony located their friends eating berries, and joined them. Leroy was the first to see them and asked how it was. Henry smiled happily and said it was very exciting, but Anthony went on and on about how he rode the bear down the mountain and saved Henry's life. Everyone looked at Henry for confirmation of Anthony's story, and Henry nodded confirmation. The guys were not convinced. Natasha looked fondly at Henry because she understood that Henry was permitting Anthony to embellish the story. Henry was a gentleman and very considerate of others.

They returned to the shade of the tree after they ate. Henry and Anthony were updated on everything that happened since they left. More and more geese had rammed trucks and cars. Andy told them that Leroy once had eaten too many berries and flew over the top of the truck to frighten the truck driver. Andy said that Leroy became so excited he nearly hit the truck. The driver saw Leroy at the last possible moment and ducked to avoid being hit. As he ducked, his hand on the steering wheel jerked the wheel and he lost control of the truck. It jack-knifed, but did not turn over. The driver was extremely upset. Leroy was embarrassed. Everyone looked at him as Andy told the story. Leroy wanted to defend himself, but he could say nothing because every word was true.

A few days later a bulldozer arrived. A man stepped out of a truck and unloaded the dozer. As soon as it was on the ground he started to destroy the shrubs. The geese did not want to abandon the berries. The dozer driver almost ran over them several times because of their reluctance to leave the berries. Some geese lowered their heads, spread their wings, hissed and charged the dozer, but it showed no fear and continued its destruction. The geese retreated a few feet and then the process was repeated again and again. Hundreds of geese watched their wonderful berries destroyed. The geese were very annoyed and disappointed.

Henry announced that he felt the Great Goose wanted him to go somewhere. He would leave early tomorrow. Anthony was surprised, as were the others. Natasha was especially sad. Anthony said he would accompany Henry because only the Great Goose knows what would happen to him if Anthony did not accompany him as his bodyguard. They were a team.

Nicholas said that his group needed to start their return to Russia but agreed that they could accompany Henry and Anthony for a while. Gilbert liked being a part of this gaggle that accepted every bird, no matter what its size or colors. Andy and Leroy had never been far from this area. Leroy tried to convince Andy to be more adventurous and Andy, finally, agreed. They would also accompany Henry and Anthony.

Andy asked Leroy to demonstrate his "Leroy Walk" in celebration of their forthcoming trip. Leroy agreed. When he finished, everyone thought his walk was creative and distinctive. Nicholas volunteered his group to do their "Caterpillar Walk." Nicholas, Dmitry, and Natasha walked to the front and lined up. First Nicholas, then Dmitry, and finally Natasha formed a tight line. They closed ranks so no light passed between them. Nicholas stood with his head held high, but Dmitry and Natasha lowered their heads. Natasha placed her head behind Dmitry's body and Dmitry placed his head behind Nicholas's body. When they were ready, they rocked to the left, to the right, and stepped out in unison, left foot first. Every step they took was as one six-footed goose: left, right, left, right. They looked like a one-headed goose with three geese bodies walking on six feet.

Eventually, the gaggle settled down and slept. They were all very excited. It would be the first time they all flew together as a gaggle, a very unusual gaggle.

The next morning they were up early. When it was time Henry and Anthony, and the others, jumped into the air and headed east. For a couple days nothing out of the ordinary happened. They were not in a hurry but flew steadily. Soon, they were over the Nebraska Sand hills where there were few houses, few ponds, and fewer trees. The only things in abundance were hills of grass rooted in hills of sand. As far as the eye could see, there was green grass.

Henry knew it was time to find a spot to spend the night. He spotted an old path that went up and around the hills. It had a fence on both sides and one short old crooked tree near the fence. They landed and found some things to eat. They eventually snuggled together at the base of the tree and began to sleep. It was tiring to fly all day.

The gaggle was sleeping near a driveway, an entrance to a small ranch. Up the road and around the bend there was a small house and barn where a rancher and his family lived. To make ends meet, the rancher drove a long-haul truck to pay the bills. He was gone for weeks at a time and then home for only a few days. But the rancher not only wanted to pay the bills, he wanted to save money so his daughters could go to college.

The rancher's life was full of sacrifices, and although his wife understood this, it was still very difficult for her. She took care of a small cow herd and moved them around from pasture to pasture. She checked and repaired fences and water tanks, water pumps and the pickup. It was hardest during calving season. She watched the cows day and night, sometimes pulling an unwilling calf from its mother. She loved the work, but she simply wanted to share it with her husband.

The problem was that her two daughters, Linda, aged 16, and Christy, aged 12, missed their Papa very much. They did not care about buying things. They wanted him to sit at the head of the table and talk to them and tell them stories so they could all laugh together. They wanted him to be at their school functions, and cheer for them when they played sports. Their mother did all she could. Sometimes she watched them play, but often she sent Linda and Christy to the event alone with the car.

Neither girl smiled or laughed much. They were used to the solitary life. They lived several miles from town on a sandy road and had few visitors at their house. They limited their excursions into town because each trip was more than a gallon of gas.

The school was in town. It was a very small school that would close soon due to declining enrollment. It was inevitable. This was ranch country. They needed several acres of pasture to support one cow. A few years ago, ranchers made a living with one hundred cows. Now, they needed a herd several times the size of their herd to make a living. Every year a rancher needed a larger cow herd, and more acres of grass, to survive.

School had just started and both girls, who were interested in extra-curricula activities, wanted to attend the organizational meetings. A few ranchers' children traveled forty or more miles to school in each direction.

When it was time to leave, their mother, Vicki, kissed each of them and told them to be careful. Linda filled the car with gas from the large overhead barrel. They climbed into the car, fastened their seat belts and drove toward the driveway. Linda was a good driver. As a rancher's daughter, she started driving tractors and the pickup before she was ten years old.

She was traveling at a normal speed and joking with her little sister, Christy; the windows were down and the early evening Sandhill breeze cooled them. The radio was playing country-western music. They rounded a turn and started downhill. The car accelerated as it continued down the hill. The driveway consisted of two sunken tire tracks with grass on each side. There were no drainage ditches. They were not needed because the sand absorbed the water as fast as Mother Nature could dump it. Several feet back from each tire track was a wire fence. Most of the fence posts were thin and leaned in one direction or another, but the corner posts were solid, especially when a gate was attached to it.

Halfway down the hill a deer burst from a gully, jumped the fence and ran in front of the car. It easily jumped the other fence and disappeared into a grassy ravine. It caught Linda by surprise and she turned the steering wheel sharply to avoid the deer. She succeeded, but abruptly left the driveway ruts, crossed the grassy area and collided with the gate. It was attached to a sturdy fence post sunk deeply into the sand. It was designed to carry the weight of the fence gate for years. After the collision, the fence post tipped, slightly, away from the car. The car stopped with its left side suspended by the post. Linda's head leaned towards her right shoulder. The car rested at a sharp angle. Neither Linda nor Christy moved. The engine stopped, but the radio still blasted country-western songs.

The gaggle woke with the deer jumping the second fence. They quickly flew back farther away from the fence before the accident. They saw the car hit the fence post. The gaggle took several steps towards the car. Henry suspected the girls were in serious trouble. He smelled gas dripping from the gas tank. Still, neither girl moved.

Henry analyzed the situation, ordered Anthony to wake the girls and make them leave the car. Only Anthony had the necessary claws to maneuver inside the car. Henry knew the girls had to leave the car for their safety. He would fly for help, but Anthony and the others had to stay with the girls, and Anthony had to find a way to make them leave the car. Henry ordered Anthony to do it fast. He said that there was no time to question. Just do it.

Henry paused to ask Anthony if he had understood. Anthony shook his head yes, but Henry wasn't convinced. Henry said, "Please, Anthony, these little girls need your help. Their lives are in your hands. You can't be afraid; you rode a grizzly bear down a mountain. This is nothing compared to that."

With that, Henry took off and followed the driveway to the highway, and then turned south towards the town.

Anthony was in shock. That was too much responsibility for a pigeon. He looked at the other birds and they motioned him to go. He flew to the window on the high side of the car. He looked at Linda and did not know what to do. He cooed. What else could a pigeon do? He cooed again and again, but Linda did not respond. He jumped onto her left shoulder and took a couple of steps towards her ear. Again, he cooed, but Linda did not move. Anthony was very frightened. He detected the smell of gasoline increasing. He rubbed his beak against her ear, but she did not move. He hopped to her right shoulder and moved towards her head. He rubbed his beak against her ear and cooed and cooed, but she did not move. Anthony was desperate. He promised Henry. He opened his beak and gently bit her ear. Nothing happened. He cooed and then he bit her ear harder and harder. Suddenly, she yelled, "Ouch!" and swatted at him knocking him from her shoulder. Anthony made a dash for the window and viewed things from a discrete tree branch.

Linda opened her eyes, confused. She slowly looked around and felt pain everywhere. She smelled gasoline and saw that Christy was not moving. She felt for her seat belt. When she found it, she released it and tried to open her door. It was heavy because she was pushing against gravity. She gathered her strength and forced it open enough to slip to the ground. Her body ached. When she released the door, gravity slammed it shut. She held her left hand to the car for balance and limped around it as best as she could until she found the other door. She opened Christy's door, reached around her, and released her seat belt. She said, "Christy, come on, sis, wake up. You have to leave this car. Come on, kiddo. Help me. Wake up."

Christy showed no sign of regaining consciousness. Linda was afraid to move her, because she did not know what injuries she had. To leave her there was a worse option. The car could become a fireball any second. She slipped one hand under Christy's legs and her other hand behind Christy's neck and head. She gently pulled her towards her chest. She struggled to stand and slowly walked to a grassy area behind the tree. She did not think she should carry her farther than that. She carefully stretched her out on the ground and began talking to her.

Anthony did not move from the safety of his branch and the others watched the scene from behind a grassy area. Within seconds, the car was on fire and black smoke poured into the sky. Linda talked to Christy, struggling not to reveal how frightened she was.

Henry continued flying toward the town. He reasoned that someone had to be there. He spotted a pickup that appeared from behind a hill. Henry tried to catch it, but could not. In Sandhill country, drivers often exceed the speed limit because there is no traffic on the roads. This pickup left Henry far behind. The town was a few miles diagonally, so Henry gave up on catching the pickup or on following the highway and turned cross-country towards the town.

Henry entered town and looked for anybody that could help. It was a small town and there were few people on the street. He flew downtown and saw no one. He swung around and flew back through town. A store clerk saw the goose fly by, opened the door and stepped out for a closer look.

Henry saw him and turned sharply to return. He landed in front of the clerk and started honking excitedly. The clerk was surprised and annoyed. Annoyance was a common reaction when a language cannot be understood, and the clerk did not understand Henry.

Henry flapped his wings and honked. The dazed clerk turned and called to someone who was deep within the store. Percy, an older gentleman and the store owner, appeared and saw Henry. He noticed Henry's white boot and approached Henry with curiosity. Henry stopped honking and flapping his wings. The store owner knelt to examine Henry's white boot. He calmly asked the clerk, "Do you have a pencil?"

The young clerk said, "Yes."

The store owner said, "Write down this number," and he read the number.

The clerk felt in his apron for paper and, when he did not find any, said, "But I don't have any paper!"

Irritated, the store owner ordered, "I don't care if you write it on the wall, on your hand, or wherever, but you will write it down right now. It is..." and he read the number. The clerk wrote it on the white paint on the door frame.

The store owner gestured for Henry to wait. The clerk scratched his head. He did not understand why the old gentleman thought he could talk with a goose.

The store owner went to the phone and yelled back at the clerk, "Now, read me those numbers slowly."

The store owner dialed the number. After a couple of rings, another old man: the Cobbler, answered. The store owner explained the situation and asked why his number was on a goose's foot. The Cobbler told him that Henry was a very special and intelligent goose. He told the store owner that Henry had recently been traveling with a pigeon. The Cobbler wrote down the store owner's phone number.

The store owner looked at Henry, and Henry looked at the store owner. Henry jumped into the sky and flew towards the car accident, although he followed the highway instead of flying diagonally. The store owner had car keys and a cell phone and walked quickly towards his car; although he did not know why he was doing it. When the highway turned north, Henry turned north. The store owner also turned north. After a few minutes, the store owner saw the smoke rising in the distance. He continued to follow Henry, but he called his clerk and told him to notify the fire department that there was a fire north of town.

The store owner did not wait for Henry. He needed to see what was burning. A fire in the sand hills can be devastating. As he turned up a driveway, he called his clerk and told him to tell the fire department that the fire was about a half mile up on the Johnson's driveway.

Within minutes, the store owner arrived at the accident scene. He saw Linda and Christy and ran to them. "Linda, honey, are you alright?"

Linda answered, "I hurt some, but I'm worried about Christy. I've been talking to her, but she doesn't hear me. Her heart is beating. She just doesn't hear me."

The store owner called the emergency service and asked for two ambulances. Within minutes a fire truck arrived and quickly doused the fire. Two firemen approached the store owner, Linda, and Christy. They had the equipment to immobilize Christy's neck and body, which they did immediately. Within another minute the first ambulance arrived and took Christy away. Minutes later, Linda was whisked away in the second ambulance. The fire truck then left to prepare for another call. The store owner continued up the driveway to inform Vicki, the rancher's wife, what had happened.

The store owner arrived and knocked on the house door. Vicki answered and showed surprise. "No one visits us unless it's an emergency," she joked. Her smile turned to a frown when the store owner did not contradict her. She said quickly, "Come in, please, and sit down. Tell me what's happened!"

He agreed and said "The girls somehow hit a fence post along the drive way. Linda appears to be fine, but Christy is unconscious. The ambulances took both of them to the hospital. If you grab your things, I can drive you there."

Seconds later they were headed back down the drive-way. When they passed the burnt car, Vicki screamed, "Were my little girls burned? Tell me now. I want to know."

The store owner used his right hand to calm her and said, "I was with both of them and I assure you they were not touched by the flames. I don't know how, but they both were safely outside the car when it caught fire."

Vicki held her right hand over her heart and muttered, "Please, God! Be with my little girls and bring them safely through this accident!"

The store owner offered Vicki his cell phone to call her husband, Jim. She accepted and called Jim's company to leave a message. She gave them the store owner's cell phone number and told them that it was an emergency. The company promised to do everything to locate him.

When they reached the hospital, Vicki jumped from the car and rushed into the hospital. "Where are my daughters? I want to see my daughters. How badly are they hurt? Please, take me to them." A nurse rushed over, and gave her a big hug. The nurse said, "Please, Vicki, sit down. I will tell you everything I know."

The nurse took Vicki's arm and led her to a sofa and sat her down. She sat beside Vicki. "This is what I know. I saw Linda brought in a wheelchair, but I think that was only a precautionary move. She seemed able to walk. She was conscious and appeared to have only a couple of small cuts. She is with Doctor Hermann now and will have some x-rays taken. Christy was brought in on a stretcher and was unconscious. I saw no bleeding anywhere. She is with Doctor Wade. She is being examined and x-rayed. Our job now is to sit, wait, and pray."

The nurse thanked the store owner for his help and told him that he could go. The store owner said that as soon as Jim called, he would notify the hospital. He left. The nurse, knowing how religious Vicki was, led her into a small non-denominational chapel. She said, "You may want to wait here. I have to stay at the front desk, but I'll come to you the second I have any more information."

Vicki slowly approached the altar, knelt and started praying.

Shortly, Doctor Hermann asked the nurse to bring Vicki in to see Linda. Vicki cried as soon as she saw Linda because she had a black and swollen eye and one arm was in a sling. They hugged, but when Vicki pulled her tight, Linda yelled with pain and pushed Vicki back from her arm. Vicki released her and added a smile and a laugh to her tears.

The doctor said, "Linda was lucky. She had her seat belt on and banged her head on the steeling wheel. She somehow sprained an arm. She should keep it in this sling for a few days and she will be fine. Don't let her ride any horses or milk any cows. Keep an eye on her, just to be safe. I don't think I need to tell you that."

Vicki asked, "What about Christy? Do you know anything yet about her?"

Doctor Hermann said that Doctor Wade was working on her and he would join him immediately."

Vicki felt better and she led Linda into the chapel where they both knelt and began to pray. The nurse walked by and saw the mother and daughter kneeling together.

The nurse prayed silently as she walked, "Please, God, find time to recognize this lovely family. They have not had much luck, but they are devoted. Please, Lord, help them overcome this difficulty. Help Christy to recover fully. Please do whatever it takes. If you must send an angel, then send your best. This family deserves no less. God, if you only listen to one prayer in my entire life, please listen to this one. Amen!"

Later, Doctor Wade sent for Vicki, and Linda. He said that Christy was still unconscious and was sent to a room in the Intensive Care Unit. She had a couple of cuts, which required a few stitches. He said that her right foot was broken and the seat belt pulled hard on her small frame and she had bruised ribs.

As for her unconsciousness, there was no specific reason found. She could regain consciousness at any time. It could be within minutes, or in years. The doctor was exact in his explanation, but Vicki gasped and put her hand in front of her mouth in surprise. She and Linda hugged each other. Linda said, "I'm sorry Mom. I didn't mean to hurt Christy. I'm so sorry. I'll never drive again."

Vicki carefully put her hand on Linda's good shoulder and said, "Honey, it's not your fault. I don't know what happened but I know it's not your fault. No matter what happens, you can never think it's your fault." Linda hugged her Mama and cried.

After a minute Linda said, "Mom, it was a deer. I was driving along and a deer jumped the fence. I swerved to miss it, and I hit the post. I'm sorry Mom."

Vicki held her as tightly as she could on Linda's good side and said, "Oh, honey, please think no more about it. Christy will be fine. You'll see. I've called for your father. He should be here soon." They returned to the chapel.

When the last ambulance had left the driveway with Linda, Henry, Anthony and the others followed it to the hospital. After Linda had disappeared inside the hospital, they went from window to window until they found the rooms where Linda and Christy were being examined. They sat and watched every movement from outside the windows; some were watching Linda while others were watching Christy. When Linda joined her mother, everyone joined and watched only Christy. When they saw a nurse removing Christy from the room, they went from window to window until they found her again. After everyone left her room, they flew to the window and sat on the windowsill and looked inside.

She looked very tiny and sad, as she lay there asleep. They thought about what they could do to help. They could not visit her in her room, so whatever they did would be from outside the window. Henry thought about Leroy and Nicholas waking the dog by pecking on the doghouse. Henry said, "Why don't we peck on the window? Maybe she will hear it and wake up." Anthony thought this was a good idea.

They started pecking frantically on the window. They made a horrible noise. The nurse opened the door to look in. She did this unexpectedly and they all had to leap from the windowsill to avoid detection.

When the nurse left again, Anthony said, "Maybe only one of us should peck at a time. We can take turns."

Henry thought this was a good idea and said he would be in the bushes nearby. When Anthony wanted to change, he could coo and Henry would come.

After awhile, Anthony cooed and Henry appeared. Anthony said, "I've tried everything and she doesn't hear anything."

Henry suggested, "Maybe she's really tired."

Anthony said, "Well, maybe, but so am I. I am off to dreamland," he jumped from the windowsill and disappeared into the bushes.

Henry was on duty now. He looked at the motionless little girl and grew sad. He pecked on the window.

After Vicki and Linda prayed, they were hungry and tired. They called the store owner, who picked them up and took them to the town café. He ate with them and had their meal placed on his tab. He took them to his house where they were given the spare bedroom. No word had been received from Jim. They were tired and quickly slept.

The next morning, the store owner's wife prepared breakfast for them. When they had eaten, she drove them to the hospital.

Vicki and Linda went directly to the nurses' station and asked for an update from Doctor Wade. They were told that he had not arrived yet, but the nurses who had been accompanying Christy had seen no change.

Vicki and Linda went to Christy's room. As they entered, they heard some noise outside the window, but when they looked there was nothing there. They put down their purses and went to her bed where they straightened Christy's hair and massaged her hands. They knelt and continued their prayers.

Within a couple of hours they received a call that Jim was on his way. The company told him to call and he called the store owner, who informed him about the accident. Jim stopped at a truck stop and called the hospital. He said that he had been on his way back when he heard about the accident. He would arrive later that day.

Vicki and Linda returned to their prayers. When Doctor Wade arrived, he stopped to see Christy. He checked her vitals and found no change. He told Vicki, "Christy seems to have simply disconnected. She has full use of all her capabilities but she has turned herself off.

The problem may not be a medical problem. She might return any minute, or never. Perhaps, when Jim arrives, all of you should come and talk to her. She may be able to hear your voices. Sometimes a person is fully conscious of happenings around them, but they are unable to make their body react to any stimuli."

Doctor Wade told them that patients with similar symptoms had suddenly returned and they knew every person who had visited them and what had been said while they had been unconscious. They could remember every detail including smells, colors and conversations. Doctor Wade asked them to be patient. He knew that with prayers and determination Christy would regain consciousness soon.

chapter

FIFTEEN

Tired of pecking the window, Henry jumped down and gave a soft honk. Anthony appeared with sleep in his eyes. Henry sighed, "It doesn't seem to be working. What can we do?"

Anthony replied sleepily, "Maybe it just takes time."

Anthony jumped back onto the windowsill to start his pecking shift. Henry flew up to look at the little girl one more time before he slept. Anthony pecked while Henry looked. The door opened unexpectedly and two ladies walked in. Henry yelled, "Jump," and they both vaulted from the windowsill.

The other members of the gaggle returned from eating. They saw the frustration on Henry and Anthony's faces. Henry said, "I don't think pecking on the window is making any difference."

Andy asked, "And you've been pecking on the window for hours, right?"

"Absolutely," said Anthony.

Nicholas offered, "Maybe she doesn't respond to sound. Could one of us enter her room and bite her real hard?"

Natasha responded harshly, "Listen to me, Nicholas. That is a little girl. Russian gentlemen geese do not bite little girls! That is cruel and stupid. Nicholas, you are a very insensitive goose." Nicholas was startled because Natasha had never criticized him, especially in front of the others, but he knew she was right.

Anthony cut into the conversation again, "Wait a minute! When I was at the car with the two girls before the ambulance arrived, I woke the bigger girl by nipping her ear. I didn't bite it hard, but gently. When she didn't wake immediately, I bit a little harder, and she woke up and tried to hit me. I flew to a tree branch and hid. She seemed angry"

Nicholas, trying to regain some respect from Natasha, replied "Yes, one of us has to go into her room and do what Anthony did in the car. Who should it be?"

Henry added, "We can't let people see us because we don't know how they'll react. It's important that none of us is seen, even in the window. Big geese are too easy to see. The smallest of us is Anthony. Anthony can go in."

Unenthusiastically, Anthony asked, "Why me? I already saved one of them, and she tried to hit me."

Henry said, "Anthony, do you see how small she is, and she is hurt. Do you think she could possibly hurt you? She can't even raise a finger. How is she going to hurt you?"

Anthony felt trapped. He didn't want to go because he distrusted people. Anthony asked, "If I go, how am I going to enter her room without being seen?"

Dmitry chimed in, "Once you enter her room, you can sit on her shoulder that is the farthest from the door. If someone enters, you can jump to the floor and hide under the chair." Everyone looked through the window to follow the logic. They all agreed.

Anthony repeated his question, "But, how am I going to enter her room?"

Henry said, "Why don't Nicholas and Dmitry go around the side and look inside the windows to see the halls? Andy and Leroy can go the other way. Natasha and I can wait here and keep an eye on the girl."

Nicholas challenged, "Why don't you and Dmitry check one side and Natasha and I will stay here?" Henry smiled foolishly as Nicholas never forgot his role as his sister's protector.

Henry cautioned, "Be careful. Remember, we can't let anyone see us. Let's meet back here in a few minutes." And they were off.

Henry and Dmitry flew low and kept a safe distance from the building. They looked inside the windows. Henry felt strange because he saw several different scenes in quick succession as he flew by the windows. He saw a person sleeping. In another room the nurse was taking a temperature. Yet, in another room, people were visiting an old man. When they reached the end of the building they turned to go around the end. From that distance they could not see inside the building so they swung around and returned much closer to the building. As they passed by the doors, they opened. Henry was surprised, yet he could remember the doors at the university that suddenly opened, and just as suddenly, they closed. He swung back for a third pass. As he passed by the door, it again opened.

Within minutes they all returned. A plan of action was quickly created. Henry explained that he could make the door open. Anthony would wait under a bush by the door and enter when it automatically opened after Henry flew by it. Henry told Anthony to be ready and enter the hospital quickly when the door opened.

When Henry mentioned flying through a door, Anthony remembered another story Henry told about going through a door. Anthony asked Henry, "Didn't you tell a story about going through a door?"

Henry said, "Yes, it was a door almost like this one. It shut suddenly and I was caught. That was when I lost my leg."

Anthony was never enthusiastic about going through the doors, but now he didn't want to go. Henry argued, "I was walking through the doors, but you will be flying. You'll be safe because the doors cannot shut fast." Anthony still felt that he was chosen because he was the smallest, which was correct.

It was time for action. The nurse was at her station when Henry flew past the door and triggered its opening, but Henry had already passed her view when she looked up and saw nothing. Anthony flew through the door like a bullet. He flew close to the nurse's station keeping the counter between him and her. He continued down the hall and landed at the end of the hallway. He peeked around the corner before flying on to the little girl's room. The geese were waiting on the windowsill and were excited when they saw him burst through the door. Leroy did his "Leroy Walk" in celebration.

Anthony flew around to the far side of the room and landed on a wooden chair. From the chair, he jumped onto her bed and, very cautiously, walked to her shoulder. He started cooing softly into her ear, and then he nibbled cautiously at her ear. If she tried to hit him, he would be able to escape quickly. He continued for several minutes with no change. Anthony looked at the others. He was crushed, as were the others. They thought that the little girl would wake, but she didn't.

Meanwhile, Leroy did the "Leroy Walk" back and forth on the sill. When he tired, Henry made faces and when he tired, the Russians did their Caterpillar Walk back and forth. There was always activity outside the window. Inside the room Anthony cooed or nibbled an ear. They tried everything.

Later, the nurse entered to check on Christy and almost caught everyone on the windowsill entertaining Christy. Anthony dived for the chair and crowded underneath as far as possible from the nurse. He could only see the nurse's legs. The Russians were Caterpillar Walking at the time and they had to dive from the windowsill. If the nurse had looked towards the window, she would have seen huge feathers still floating in the air.

The nurse checked the equipment, but Christy's condition had not changed. The nurse knew that Christy was somewhere, and that she was sad because her face had a frown.

When the nurse left, Henry jumped up and continued his pecking, smiling and face-making. He motioned for Anthony to return to work, also. Instead of returning to Christy, Anthony flew to the inside of the window and tried to tell Henry that he wanted out. He was afraid. He wanted Henry to open the front door because he was coming out. Anthony turned and flew out the door. Henry understood and jumped from the windowsill and hurried to fly near the front door. The door opened, the nursed looked and saw nothing, and then Anthony shot through and followed Henry back to the group.

When they arrived at the windowsill again, they noticed that the little girl was smiling. They noticed that her smile seemed connected to Leroy's special moves in his "Leroy Walk." Henry was the first to notice. He told Leroy to stop. Leroy did, but he looked at Henry not understanding. The girl stopped smiling. Henry signaled Leroy to start again. Leroy smiled and picked up where he had left off. Henry watched the girl and she again smiled.

Henry called to Leroy to stop and let the Russians back on stage. Everyone looked at Henry for an explanation. He said, "She doesn't have her eyes open and she doesn't seem to hear us, but she knows what we're doing, and she likes it." Henry continued, "Nicholas, take Dmitry and Natasha and do the caterpillar walk, and we'll see if she reacts." They did, and her smile reappeared.

And the joy seemed to return to the group. The girl's smile made them want to show her everything they knew. Henry had Anthony jump onto his back and he flew back and forth with Anthony on his back. Henry wanted to do more, so he swung around and gained altitude. With an unsuspecting Anthony, he dove towards the ground. Anthony dug in his claws as he held on for his life. They were driving straight to earth when Henry reversed his direction and swung upwards. This was very difficult because he had to reverse his weight and that of Anthony's weight. Anthony was silent, not because he was not terrified, but because any sounds he made he was swallowing. Henry thrust the two of them up and rolled over to complete the 360 degree loop.

The group was almost intoxicated with excitement when Henry and Anthony returned. When they landed, Anthony had his claws dug deep into Henry's back and appeared frozen. Henry, feeling Anthony's claws waited a second for him to dismount. When he did not, Henry raised high on his legs and flapped his wings dispelling Anthony. The group was very happy, but they wanted the girl to wake up. Smiling was good, but awake was better. Unnoticed, Anthony had not moved and was frowning at Henry. He was not celebrating.

An eighteen-wheeler pulled up and stopped in front of the hospital. Its diesel engine roared, the air-brakes released, and the engine fell silent. When Henry heard the eighteen-wheeler, he froze. The others noticed his reaction and asked what had happened. Henry told them about his first experience with such a truck when he was gliding in front of it. He told how the horn blew and the sound of the brakes screamed; how he was caught on the windshield wipers and, when he thought he was going to die, he was tossed free.

Jim stepped quickly from the truck, and as he hurried towards the front door, Vicki and Linda rushed towards him. They hugged for a second and then entered the hospital. Jim went first, and almost caught the geese in the middle of their celebration.

Jim kissed Christy and stroked her hair. He said, "Vicki, look, Christy is smiling." Vicki and Linda each took a step closer and saw that it was true.

Vicki exclaimed, "She wasn't smiling before. Linda, call the nurse. Jim, I swear, she wasn't smiling before."

Jim grabbed Christy's hand and begged, "Kitten, please come back to us, honey. We need you. This is Papa. I'm home, kitten. Please come back."

They were surprised when they heard her giggle. Her smile and giggle surprised everyone as she rarely smiled, and never giggled. The nurse rushed in with Linda. They heard Christy's giggle before they saw her smile. The nurse threw her hands up to her mouth in surprise, and tears came to her eyes. She said, "I'll call Doctor Wade. She may be coming back. I think she's coming back."

Before the nurse could reach for a phone to call Doctor Wade, Christy's eyes fluttered. Jim called, "Please come back, baby. We love you. We need you. Please honey."

Within seconds, Christy opened her eyes and looked around. She said, "Hi Papa. Hi Mama. Where am I? What happened?" They hugged her and cried.

Every member of the international gaggle was on the windowsill, looking in, and crying also. They rubbed each other's necks and beaks and had a very emotional moment. Henry tried to snuggle next to Natasha, but he couldn't pass Leroy without falling from the sill. Then Christy spotted them and pulled away from her hugs and pointed excitedly towards the window, "There they are! They're real! There they are! Mama, Papa, look!" It was impossible for Jim or Vicki to look fast enough to see anything, except a falling feather. The gaggle had already jumped from the sill. Each member of the gaggle landed in a pile on the ground. They tried not to squawk, but it was painful.

Jim and Vicki looked towards the window for a moment, and then returned to look inquisitively at Christy. "What was it, honey?" asked Jim.

Christy asked, "Didn't you see them?"

Vicki said, "See who, dear?"

Christy said, "You didn't see the birds in the window?"

Jim and Vicki looked at each other. Vicki said, "No, honey. We didn't. I'm sorry."

"But Mama, they were just there! Now they're gone. Mama, make them come back."

"Make who come back, honey?" asked Jim.

"The birds, Papa, the birds," cried Christy, frustrated.

At that moment, Doctor Wade arrived. He walked to Christy, and as he grabbed Christy's hand to check her pulse, he said, "Good to see you made it safely, Jim. Now, how are you feeling, Christy?"

Christy paused before answering. She answered slowly, "I'm sore all over and my head hurts, but I'm fine. How come no one else can see the birds?"

"What birds have you seen, Christy?" asked Doctor Wade.

"I think some are geese. One is smaller and others are very large."

"Do you know the names of the birds, honey?" asked Jim.

"The regular-sized ones look like Canada geese, but I've never seen any of the others before," said Christy.

Doctor Wade said that Christy had to rest and everyone had to leave. The doctor followed them out of the room and closed the door behind him.

Jim, Vicki, and Linda went to a restaurant to eat and talk. They were very worried about Christy seeing birds that no one else could see. As a precaution, Jim thought they should go to the library and look for a book with photographs of birds. They could show it to Christy and maybe, if she was really seeing birds, she could identify which ones she saw.

Instead of sleeping, Christy fixed her eyes on the window. Within minutes, Anthony jumped back onto the windowsill. He started marching back and forth on the sill like a soldier on-guard. Then, he gave his rendition of the "Leroy Walk" in each direction. Christy again giggled and laughed. After Anthony's act came the Russians and then Leroy.

When Jim, Vicki, and Linda returned to the hospital with a large book filled with bird photographs, they were surprised to find that Christy had not slept. They showed her the book and asked her to point to any birds she had seen in the window. She started turning the pages slowly. She asked, "Mama, can birds be angels?"

"Why do you ask?" said Vicki.

"I'm just wondering. That's all," said Christy. She continued to turn the pages slowly. She suddenly stopped turning pages and asked, "Do birds have different colored feet?"

Vicki asked, "Do birds have different colored feet? I don't think they can, unless it's a mutation. Are you sure you're feeling alright?"

"Yes, Mama, I feel fine. One of the Canada geese has a black foot and a white foot," replied Christy. She continued, "Mama, do you know if there is a bird that rides on the back of another bird when it flies?"

At this point, Vicki asked Christy to excuse her and Papa. She asked Linda to talk with Christy while Vicki and Jim stepped outside into the hallway.

Once they were safely outside the door, "Jim," Vicki said, "When Percy went to our house to tell me about the accident, he mentioned a goose that had flown into town and attracted his clerk's attention. Percy followed the goose. When he went north on the highway, he saw our car on fire. He was the one who called the fire trucks and ambulances to save our kids. He never saw the goose again"

Jim asked, "Do you think the goose took Percy to the accident site on purpose?"

Vicki answered, "I have no idea. When Percy arrived at the accident, Linda and Christy were already safely out of the car."

Jim asked, "Did you ask Linda how she was able to pull Christy from the car?"

Vicki answered, "No, I didn't think to ask. Everything happened so fast. I'll go in to talk with Christy and send Linda out to you, and you can ask her."

Vicki returned to the room and sent Linda out. As Linda entered the hallway, she asked, "What is it Papa? Is everything alright?"

Jim asked, "Honey, how were you able to pull Christy from the car right after the accident?"

Linda seemed surprised. She paused before answering, "Papa, it's not really clear to me. I think I was unconscious right after the accident." She tried to remember the sequence of events. "This may sound strange, Papa, but I remember a sound in my ear, a whisper or something, and then I felt a sharp pain in my ear, and I awoke and smelled gasoline. I knew I had to leave the car and pull Christy from it. Why do you ask, Papa?"

Jim replied, "Oh, no reason, honey. Come here. I want to see something." She approached and he examined her ears. He found two or three minor cuts, on her right ear. He said, "Alright, Kitten, let's go back in and see how Christy's doing."

As Christy continued through the pages, she stopped and said, "This is the same bird, Papa. What is a Homing Pigeon?"

They looked, and Christy was pointing at the photograph of a Homing Pigeon. Within minutes she had also identified a Mallard Duck and confirmed the Giant Canada geese. Christy said, "But I can't find the really big birds. I don't see them anywhere."

Doctor Wade returned to check on Christy. Jim said, "Christy has identified one of the birds as a Homing Pigeon, another as a Mallard Duck, and three or four as Giant Canada geese. She hasn't yet found a photograph of the biggest bird. What bird is bigger than a Giant Canada Goose?

Doctor Wade thought a moment and replied, "Isn't an eagle larger than a goose? I don't know. A turkey is also larger, isn't it?"

Later, Christy stopped suddenly and yelled, "Here are the big ones! Here they are!"

Christy positively identified the last birds as Tula geese. Christy added that they were from Russia. They were Russian geese.

Jim summarized, "So, you have seen a Homing Pigeon, a Mallard Duck, several Giant Canada Geese and Russian Geese. Is that correct?"

Christy confirmed his summary, and then asked, "Mama, can you find the geese? I want to take them home."

Vicki replied, "Kitten, I don't know how we could find the geese. And if we do, I don't know how we could capture them. You must remember, these are wild birds and they should not be held captive."

Doctor Wade said that Christy needed to rest again. He suggested that the Johnson family also rest and return the next day. They said their good-byes and left.

They went to visit Percy. They asked him if he knew anything about one bird flying on another bird's back. He did not. They asked him if he knew anything about a bird with one white foot and one black foot. Percy was surprised and told them about the white boot on the foot of the goose that visited him. He told them how he found the telephone number and called it and a Cobbler answered from a town three hours away. Jim and Vicki told Percy what Christy had told them. They were all surprised, but more so when Percy mentioned that the Cobbler had said that goose with the white boot had been traveling with a pigeon.

The day came for Christy to return home. They were excited until Jim said that he would have to leave that afternoon for more loads with his truck. Christy and Linda lost their smiles and nearly cried. They wanted their papa to be near them. The nurse entered and asked Jim and Vicki to see the doctors before they left.

Jim and Vicki went to Doctor Wade's office. Doctor Hermann was also present. Doctor Wade sat at his desk and Doctor Hermann leaned against the wall. He stood on one foot with the other pressed against the wall. They both were smiling and were having a good day. Doctor Wade asked them to sit. He spoke of the miracle of Christy's recovery. He said that he never expected anything as complete and rapid. He said that she improved rapidly after Jim and Vicki were both present.

He asked them to forgive him for his presumptuousness, but he had a couple of full-time jobs that needed filling. He thought that they might be interested in them. They were not very high paying jobs, but they were important, and Jim and Vicki would have full medical coverage. One position was for a janitor/handyman. The hours were flexible, and could be worked out in advance for each week. The other was a nurse's aide position. The hours were less flexible, but would be negotiated on an 'as-needed' basis. The doctors would pay for college courses for her to receive her LPN license. They discussed the salaries, and Jim and Vicki accepted without hesitation.

They returned to collect the girls to go home. Jim and Vicki sat the girls down and gave them the news. The girls smiled like Jim and Vicki had never seen them smile. They smiled so wide that they almost swallowed their ears. Jim cautioned that he would have to give his two-weeks notice before he could stay at home full-time, but the smiles did not disappear.

Percy arrived with his large car to give Vicki, Linda and Christy a ride to their ranch. He parked in front of the hospital and opened the doors. They all entered the car and prepared for the ride home.

The international gaggle watched from the bushes. They were aware that they had succeeded. Henry said, "Anthony hop on. Everyone else form on my right wing. We are going to say goodbye to the girls."

Henry and the others jumped into the sky and quickly overtook the car. They accompanied it on the left side. Henry and Anthony were the farthest from the car. On Henry's right wing followed Gilbert, Andy, Leroy, Natasha, Dmitry, and Nicholas. They all looked straight ahead until they were certain they had been seen. Simultaneously, they looked towards the car and each goose gave its best smile and honk. They followed as best as they could, but when the car began to pull away, they banked and turned away.

Christy asked, "Mama, can I raise geese at home? You know, Mama, I think I will be a veterinarian when I go to college."

Jim, witnessing the goose salute, had a flashback to a few months ago when he was driving on Interstate 80. A goose became stuck on his windshield, and he received a ticket for reckless driving.

chapter

SIXTEEN

Tom, Doug, and Rich had been friends since they were five years old. They were together during every year of school from kindergarten to their senior year in high school. They were very athletic and practiced every sport, but they had been best in football. They were widely known as the region's triple-threat in football. Tom was the quarterback, Doug was the half-back, and Rich was the wide receiver. They were feared by all opponents and respected by their schoolmates and local citizens. That was twenty-two years ago.

Since then, they added a few pounds to their frame. Their belt buckles were no longer visible because their muscles had softened and fallen, covering their belts. They still considered themselves the triple threat, but no one paid attention to them. Each married and had children. None went to college. They stayed in the town of their fame and found work. Tom was a telephone repairman. Doug worked in the lumber yard. Rich worked in the grain elevator.

During the day, they worked at their jobs. At night, they usually met at a bar where they talked about two things: their famous days as the triple threat, and hunting. They were avid hunters. They hunted pheasants, quail, ducks, geese, deer, and anything that moved. Sometimes they shot targets. Anything served as a target. A tree, a post, a bottle, a can, a dirt clod, a stick in the river—anything served.

They were mediocre hunters and frequently returned without game, but they always had a good time. Doug had a hunting dog: a Black Labrador named Dodger. He took pride in personally training the dog. Dodger ran after balls, sticks, and rubber birds. The three hunters did not always remember to buy hunting licenses, and they were known to hunt outside the legal hunting season. They usually took whiskey with them to keep warm. Nebraska could be very cold, especially when the north winds were blowing. It could also be very warm if the south winds were blowing, and beer would help to keep them from overheating.

Last spring, Doug negotiated an agreement with a retired farmer who owned land on the south side of the Platte River. If Doug sprayed and cut the thistles in the pasture that bordered the river; he and his friends could hunt on the river and build a hunting blind.

Doug went to the site to decide where the hunting blind should be built. There were two or three places under consideration. He asked his partners to help make a final selection.

On Saturday, they loaded the pickup with Dodger, a case of beer, and their shotguns and went to the river. They parked the pickup, opened a beer and started walking around discussing the pros and cons of each site. They looked like engineers preparing to build a new bridge across the Platte River. Dodger was busy sniffing trees and following invisible paths that were made by rabbits or deer. After they drank a few more beers, they made their final site selection.

The next question was how to build the blind and who would supply the materials. This was a significant project that would take many weekends and require lots of beer to complete.

The construction started the following weekend. They built the blind a few feet back from the river, a foot higher than the bank and behind some brush. They each sipped on a beer and used a spade to level the area. There was more sipping on beer than there was leveling of the area. Within a few minutes, their concept of level became more flexible.

Rich unenthusiastically trimmed brush, but kept a beer in his hand. Doug and Tom marked the area for the blind and started framing it. Much was expected of Doug because he worked in a lumberyard, but he had as much difficulty following a saw-line as the others. Fortunately, the construction of a hunting blind did not require precision work.

Once the frame was constructed, they added old boards to the walls and the roof. The material had to be old to help camouflage the blind. New boards were bad because the birds would be suspicious of the bright wood and not land nearby. Inside, they placed several shelves. The shelves were for their bar, the gas heater, the radio and TV, a gaslight and a library, which consisted of several magazines with abundant photographs and few words.

They put wooden shutters in front and on the sides so that when the birds approached, they could quickly pop out with their shotguns and surprise the birds.

It was becoming a beautiful blind. After three weekends, they stepped back, patted each other on the back and popped the top on a new beer. Doug gave a short toast. They all took long gulps while gazing at their masterpiece. The sound of their gulping was heard by birds for at least fifty yards.

It would be magnificent hunting when the season opened in a couple of months. There was only one thing left to do. Rich, the avid reader of the group, had read an article in the paper about the Department of Transportation in California. They had to destroy shrubs that were planted near an interstate highway. The problem was that the bushes produced a berry that geese ate, and it had alcoholic content. The geese became intoxicated. Rich thought they might give them an edge over the birds if the birds were intoxicated. Rich called and discovered the name of the shrub. He found a local nursery that had them in inventory and ordered a pickup load of them. They planted them in a semi-circle behind the blind. They carried a few buckets of water from the river to ensure that the plants would not become thirsty.

During the next six to eight weeks, they visited the blind every weekend. They watered the shrubs, which grew rapidly. They sat inside the blind with the windows open, sipped beer and imagined the ducks and geese arriving for them to shoot. When hunting season opened in a few weeks, they would take home their limit every day. They would again be known as "the triple threat."

Each week they become more anxious. They began to see more and more ducks and geese traveling the skies with each new weekend. They now had a fully stocked bar, a complete library, gas lamps, and a gas refrigerator. They were ready. They were preparing to go home when they saw a couple of geese circling.

It was more temptation than they could resist. They excitedly touched each other's shoulder and ran for their shotguns. They each loaded three shells and stood behind the blind. When the geese started to land, they opened fire and two geese dropped like lead weights into the river. Doug ordered Dodger to fetch. Dodger had no idea what he was expected to do. He barked and looked around, expecting Doug to throw a stick into the river. Doug and Rich quickly ran down stream and secured the geese. They washed them off in the river, dropped them into a gunny sack and threw the sack inside the tool box that was behind the pickup cab. They returned to Doug's house and went into the garage where they cleaned the geese in privacy.

During that week, Doug realized that they had no duck or geese decoys. Decoys were expensive and they could not buy them because their collective discretionary hunting income would not permit such an extravagance. The best alternative was to build decoys from blocks of wood. This was inexpensive but it required a big investment in work. The three hunters did have the time, but they did not like to work.

Doug stated the obvious, "Well, we don't have the money to buy any, do we? We don't have time to make any, do we?"

Rich asked impatiently, "Well, Einstein, what do you suggest?"

Doug was ready for the question and responded, "Dodger is black, isn't he? Well, we can smudge some white makeup on his face to make him look like a Canada goose, can't we? And we can put some stuff on his back and belly to do the same. How smart are those geese anyways? They probably can't see very well from very far. They won't know that Dodger isn't a goose. I can throw a stick into the water and when he goes to retrieve it, the geese will think he's a goose. And they'll think its safe and land."

Tom and Rich were not yet convinced, but they thought about it. Rich said, "Let's do a dry run today. We can paint Dodger and then Doug can throw the stick into the water and we will see if it will work." Everyone agreed to meet at the blind by mid-afternoon.

Rich, always late, arrived when Doug and Tom were on their second beer. Doug called Dodger, who was out scouting the area for scents. When he pranced nearby, Doug grabbed Dodger. Dodger knew that something was up when Doug tied him to the pickup bumper. Dodger did not know what was going to happen, but he guessed it was not going to be fun.

Doug started painting the sides of Dodger's face white, while Rich did the back and Tom did the undercarriage. They had to step back a few times before applying some additional makeup here and there. Within minutes, they were done. They stepped back and admired their work. Dodger whined, put his tail between his legs, and sat down. His eyes begged an end to whatever they were doing. They laughed and opened another beer. Dodger crawled under the truck and refused to come out.

Doug found a stick to throw, but Dodger had to be coaxed from under the truck. Tom and Rich grabbed their shotguns and stood next to the blind. Each placed his beer on a ledge in the blind. When Dodger saw the stick, he overcame his embarrassment and ran to Doug's side. Doug threw the stick as far as he could into the river and Dodger leapt to retrieve it. While Dodger happily swam for the stick, Doug grabbed his shotgun and set his beer down.

At that moment, Henry decided to take the gaggle down for the evening to rest on the river. As they came in they saw the dog in the river, but none of them thought anything of it and continued their approach.

When the "triple threat" saw the geese arrive, they thought it was an offering from God. They reasoned that it would be sinful to waste such an opportunity.

They looked at each other, nodded, and raised their shotguns to take aim. As the geese drew nearer, the triple threat each pumped three shots, and one bird dropped into the weeds just slightly downstream.

The geese were surprised. Henry honked orders as they broke their descent and sped off. They looked and Gilbert was missing. Henry dispatched Andy and Leroy to find and defend him. They broke from formation and returned to find Gilbert. They flew very low, upstream from east to west. When they approached Gilbert's location, they landed on the river's edge and started walking. They honked very softly hoping that Gilbert would answer. He did. They went to him and saw that the river's current had carried him into some brush where he was not easily visible. The brush prevented the river's current from taking him downstream. He could not be pulled away from the bank by the same current. Andy and Leroy took positions on each side of Gilbert.

Henry landed the group a short distance away and nervously said, "Hunting season must have started. I'm sorry. I didn't think about that. I should have known when I saw the dog. Let's find out how Gilbert is. If he can fly, we'll move him to a safer area."

Nicholas was of a different opinion. He said angrily, "This river is beautiful and it should be a nice place to rest. I think we should stay here as long as we like."

Henry argued, "Nicholas, do you remember your promise that you made to your Mama and Papa about protecting Natasha and Dmitry?"

Nicholas was not in a forgiving mood. Nicholas countered, "Why don't we do to them what we did to the hunter at the berry patch? They should be smart enough to leave and never return if we hit them like we did the hunter at the berry patch."

Henry was unsure, but said, "I'll fly near them and see how many there are of them and then we will make a plan." Before anyone could comment, he was in flight.

Meanwhile, Dodger had returned with the stick and Doug ordered him to retrieve the duck he had shot. Dodger only wanted Doug to throw the stick again. Finally, in frustration, Doug threw the stick into the area where he thought the duck was hiding. Dodger sped towards the stick.

Andy and Leroy saw and heard the stick fall only a couple of feet away from them. Leroy said to Andy, "I have first chance at the dog. You stay with Gilbert." Andy gave a soft honk in agreement.

Dodger came after the stick and Leroy hissed and flapped his wings. Dodger had a memory lapse, forgot he was retrieving a stick, and turned to run. In doing so, he presented Leroy with a long tail, which Leroy could not resist. Leroy grabbed the tail and clamped down hard. Dodger yelped and took off running as fast as he could upstream. Leroy started gliding over the water as carefully positioned his webbed feet to slide on the water surface. Leroy was waterskiing. If he could have honked in happiness, he would have, but he had to keep his beak closed.

Dodger continued to accelerate. Leroy extended his wings and began to glide above the water. Dodger had to turn left to reach the river's bank and his owner. As Dodger changed direction, Leroy quickly took up any slack before he also had to change direction. The force of Leroy's momentum caused Dodger to tip his hindquarters. He righted himself and ran towards his owner, yelping for help.

As Dodger came closer to the bank, Tom yelled, "When he reaches the bank, shoot the goose."

Doug quickly yelled back, "Don't you dare shoot my dog. The way you shoot, you'd miss the goose and hit my dog. Don't anybody shoot."

When the dog hit the river's edge, Leroy felt it wise to take flight and return to Andy and Gilbert.

Doug examined Dodger's tail as Dodger cried from pain. They all heard a goose honking from behind. It came from the trees in the pasture. They turned around and pointed their guns, but they could see no goose. They could only hear the constant honking, which came closer and closer and then grew weaker.

Once Henry was on the other side, he looped back by selecting a route farther from the river's bank. When he reached Anthony and the Russian geese, he said that there were three hunters. Henry continued, "Nicholas and Dmitry should go north, fly low over the river and turn south to come straight in towards the hunters. I can go through the woods and honk. That will make the hunters turn their backs toward the river, and you can safely hit them."

Anthony protested, "Yeah, and they'll shoot at you. Who's going to protect you while Nicholas and Dmitry aim at the hunters?"

Henry replied with confidence, "I can fly fast, low, and around trees. They cannot hit me. Anthony, you and Natasha stay here." Henry turned towards Nicholas and Dmitry and said seriously, "Watch the men and do not miss. Do not attack unless they have their backs turned towards you. Are we ready? Let's go." And they were off.

Henry made a quick loop to gain speed and allow Nicholas and Dmitry time to enter into position. Henry flew as fast as he could and honked constantly. The triple threat turned around to face the direction from which the honks were coming. Their guns rested on their shoulders, ready to aim and fire as soon as they saw anything, but they did not see anything. They could only hear that goose again.

Meanwhile, Nicholas and Dmitry approached rapidly. They selected the hunter in the middle as their target and overlapped wings. As they hit Tom, he flipped forward before he hit the ground. When he was hit by the geese, the force knocked his gun barrel toward the ground and it fired, hitting Rich in the foot. Rich yelled in pain and said, "You twit. You shot me. Why did you shoot me? I'm not the goose. Do I look like a goose?"

As Rich yelled, Nicholas and Dmitry gained a few feet of altitude after impact and then dropped in behind the trees. Doug and Rich did not see the Russian geese.

Tom was flat on the ground with his arms and legs extended in all directions. He was not sure what had happened. He thought he was in a football game again and had just been tackled. He looked up and saw two huge birds disappearing on the horizon. He sat straight. As he held himself up with one hand, Dodger approached him and licked his face several times. He only said, "What the beep was that? What happened?" as he pushed Dodger away.

Doug yelled, "You dumb twit. You shot Rich in the foot. That's what happened! What were you thinking? What are you doing on the ground?" Neither Doug nor Rich had seen the Russian geese.

Nicholas and Dmitry swung around while Henry also repositioned for another pass. Henry was honking continuously. The triple threat was mad. Doug was tired of that goose taunting them. Tom still sat on the ground feeling the back of his neck and Rich held his foot while cursing at Tom.

Doug caught a glimpse of Henry flying low and he emptied his shotgun. He did not hit Henry, but he knocked out one headlight, one windshield, and one radiator. Tom stood and shot repeatedly. He flattened one tire, and hit one leaky gas tank. Doug was the best shot of the triple threat.

Doug swore, and reloaded as he surveyed the damage to their trucks. Rich tried to stand. Nicholas and Dmitry hit Tom again from behind. He spun again, but when his gun fired, it hit another radiator.

Rich yelled, "Darn, you guys! What are you fools doing? You shot me in the foot and now you're killing our trucks. Come on! They're just geese!"

Tom was again stretched out on the ground. He was not sure what had happened. He sat up and clapped his hands together and yelled, "Come on you guys. We can still win this game!

Afraid that these tactics would not work a third time, Henry started a low flight from southeast to northwest on the bank near the blind. Doug and Rich heard him coming and aimed towards the sound. When they saw him, they unloaded their weapons. They did not hit Henry, as he did his "corkscrew maneuver," but they did hit their hunting blind. They destroyed their bar, their TV and radio, and their gaslight, which now burned rapidly. The fire spread to the library, and when it touched the remains of their bar, the blind was quickly encompassed with flames and smoke.

Henry swung around and flew from northwest to southeast and came from the river towards the blind. When Anthony saw this, he was sure that Henry's luck had ended. He threw himself into the air and flew near the pickup, almost in the opposite direction to Henry. He was much closer to the hunters than Henry. Anthony hoped to confuse the hunters and make it harder for them to hit anything. It worked as they unloaded their weapons, again hitting the trucks several times. Another tire was flat and a spark was generated that hit the leaking gasoline. They heard a puff, and the truck was engulfed in flames. The sky was filling with smoke, belching from the burning truck and hunting blind.

Dmitry and Nicholas returned to the waiting gaggle, as did Henry and Anthony.

Doug went to the two pickups that were not burning and looked for something to fight the truck fire. The hunting blind was already beyond salvation. He could not find anything. The burning truck finally exploded when the flames reached the gas tank. Doug and Tom pushed the other two trucks back several feet to keep them from catching fire.

They all heard the sirens from a fire truck and police cars quickly approaching. The firemen arrived and put out the fires. The policemen arrived and started asking questions. They wanted to know how the fires had started and who had shot Rich. "Well," Rich said, "It all started when they sent their hunting dog to retrieve the duck."

The policeman, puzzled, asked, "What duck?"

Rich, not realizing the potential for a problem, replied happily, "There was a duck and some geese flying and we shot the duck. He fell right over there" as he pointed to some bushes.

The policeman replied incredulously, "But hunting season hasn't started yet. May I see your hunting licenses?" When he saw Dodger, he asked, "And what is this?"

Doug said, "We didn't have any decoys, so we made him into a living decoy."

With that, the triple threat was in the 'dog house.' The policeman read them their rights and placed handcuffs on each of them.

The triple threat was charged with hunting out of season, hunting without a license, intoxication while hunting, and inhumane treating of an animal. They were taken first to the hospital for emergency treatment and then to the police station. Their wives were called. Justice would be handed out and it would be swift and harsh.

After the police and firemen left, the gaggle went to visit Gilbert. His wing had been damaged. He could walk, but he could not fly. Henry asked Andy and Leroy to stay and protect Gilbert. Henry would take the others to meet his friend. They would return as soon as possible with help.

Henry and the others took to flight and headed south. After a half hour, Henry swung the gaggle toward the town, over the park, and along Main Street to the fountain, and the Cobbler. Their arrival caused many heads to turn. They went to the fountain and started swimming, except for Anthony. He stayed on the fountain's edge. Anthony still did not like water.

Henry discretely went to the Cobbler's back door, pecked three times and waited. Within a few seconds, the door opened and the Cobbler, surprised, knelt to look more closely at Henry. Henry was nervous and honked in a strange manner. He looked directly into the Cobbler's eyes, honked, and then took a few steps back. He kept repeating the process.

The Cobbler collected his car keys, locked the shop's door and walked to his car, which was parked nearby. As soon as he started his car, Henry took to flight. Henry led the Cobbler through the streets to the highway. People stopped to gawk at the strange sight.

Henry led on, as they traveled north. Oncoming traffic applied brakes as they passed the goose-led car. They turned off the road and followed a path to the river's edge. Henry landed by the damaged truck and the remains of the hunting blind. The Cobbler, confused, looked at Henry wondering what Henry had to do with the damage. Henry started walking through the brush and honked as he walked. The Cobbler followed. After a couple minutes, the Cobbler saw Andy, Leroy and Gilbert. The Cobbler stopped and stood absolutely still. Henry honked. Andy and Leroy honked. Gilbert did not honk. He only looked at the Cobbler. Gilbert, Andy and Leroy did not like humans.

The Cobbler waited for a sign that he could move to help. He waited while Henry and the others talked. The Cobbler saw that it was Gilbert who was hurt. The Cobbler guessed that the truck and hunting blind remnants had something to do with the problem.

Henry continued to honk softly. He took a few more steps towards Andy, Leroy and Gilbert. Andy, Leroy, and Gilbert looked at Henry, then at the Cobbler and back at Henry. Finally, Henry turned towards the Cobbler and honked. Andy and Leroy did not move, but Gilbert took a step towards the Cobbler. He looked to Henry for reassurance and then towards the Cobbler for any sign of betrayal. Gilbert took a few more steps. The Cobbler took a couple of short steps and knelt. Gilbert took more steps until the Cobbler could reach him. Finally, the Cobbler picked up Gilbert very carefully. He saw that one wing was severely damaged.

The Cobbler, carefully carrying Gilbert, and Henry returned to the car. The Cobbler opened the passenger door and put Gilbert on the floor. He stepped back and made a gesture towards Henry. Henry jumped in and sat beside Gilbert. Andy and Leroy already circled overhead.

The Cobbler drove carefully so his passengers would not be frightened anymore. As he drove, he heard Henry honking and squawking very softly. Gilbert looked constantly at the Cobbler. He still did not trust humans.

The Cobbler drove directly to the veterinarian clinic and opened the door. He did not wait for his passengers to step out. He ran into the clinic and within a minute he returned for Gilbert. He carefully secured him and removed him from the car. A helper appeared and held the door open. They all entered, except for Henry.

Henry did not know what to do. He was very anxious. He returned to the fountain and honked to the remainder of his gaggle. They all took flight and followed him back to the clinic. They sat at the edge of the parking lot. Sometimes they sat and sometimes they walked. It seemed like hours, then the clinic door opened and the Cobbler appeared with Gilbert, who had a bandaged wing.

The Cobbler was surprised to see so many birds waiting. He knew he should not try to approach them, so he knelt and sat Gilbert on the pavement. Henry honked and hurried over. Henry used his beak to rub on Gilbert's neck. Gilbert said, "My wing doesn't hurt now. I don't know what they did, but it feels much better. I know I cannot fly. Perhaps, I should trust this man for a while and see what happens. So far, he has only helped me."

Henry agreed. Henry knew that the Cobbler would only help Gilbert.

Anthony cooed at Gilbert and the other geese honked, but they kept their distance.

The Cobbler carefully put Gilbert on the floor in the passenger side and returned to the back of his shop. The others followed and landed nearby. The Cobbler took Gilbert inside, where he fed him and gave him water. Gilbert was given a comfortable area to rest. When the Cobbler finished, he took some corn and other seeds out and placed them at the base of the fountain. Henry and his friends hurried to eat. They were very hungry.

chapter

SEVENTEEN

Each day Henry and the others were given corn. The Cobbler always brought Gilbert out to eat with Henry and the others. They ate heartily and exchanged honks. It was a ritual that several local citizens began to monitor. They were impressed with the oddity of this strange gaggle. They had never seen a duck, a pigeon, and Canada geese together. They had never seen Tula geese. They had no idea what they were, but the citizens found them interesting.

When the mini-gaggle finished the corn and decided it was time to go to the park for some grass, they formed their line and marched off. The Cobbler placed Gilbert in a cardboard box, with a window cut into the front, and then placed the box on a handcart with large soft tires. He followed the geese down the street to the park. Henry, Gilbert and the others were very vocal on the trip. This caused many storeowners, clerks, and customers to step outside and watch the parade.

After a half hour, the Cobbler returned with Gilbert to his store. Gilbert needed to rest and the Cobbler needed to work. Gilbert was placed behind the counter and on the other side of a doorway where he was always seen by the Cobbler. The Cobbler ensured that Gilbert did not feel threatened by the customers.

Henry and his mini-gaggle met and mingled with the other gaggle that also utilized the fountain and the park. Andy and Leroy mingled among the lady geese, which had recently lost their ganders. In fact, two ganders had recently gone to the river, and they never returned. No one knew what had happened. They simply disappeared.

Andy and Leroy were very courteous and helpful, although the young widows were still in mourning and did not return their attentions.

Nicholas, Dmitry, and Natasha rested and ate as much as they could. They loved the corn and visibly increased in size.

Anthony stayed close to Henry. He felt out of his element. There were so many geese around him, and only one Anthony. He was tired of geese pointing their beaks at him and honking to each other. He knew he was discussed. He heard some geese speculating what kind of goose he was. Some referred to him as the 'runt goose,' which made

Anthony furious. He did not like the other geese. He only liked those in his mini-gaggle.

Henry became restless. He asked Nicholas, "When are you thinking of returning to your family?"

Nicholas replied, "Soon, very soon. We must become very strong first as the flight is very long and very difficult."

Henry asked, "What direction will you fly to reach home?"

Nicholas said, "We will fly to the northeast for about four or five days. When we reach the ocean, we must rest a couple of days and eat well. Then we must fly over the ocean to an island. Then we fly again over the ocean to another island. Finally, we fly over ocean and then we fly only over land. I think it could take two weeks to reach home. We must be careful and rest and eat on the islands."

Henry paused a moment and then asked, "Nicholas, would you mind if I accompany you? I have never been there and it might be interesting. I would love to see your home and family. For some reason I feel I need to go with you."

Anthony overheard and interrupted, "Henry, if you go, then I also will go. You and I are a team. You know that without my protecting your back, only bad things will happen to you."

Henry again became thoughtful. He liked Anthony, but he was afraid that this trip may be too rough for the little guy. "Do you think you can make the trip, Anthony? Can you keep up with us? You heard how long it will take and how difficult it can be?"

Henry did not want to leave without Anthony. It seemed they had been friends, forever.

Anthony said, "I'm little, but I can fly all of you into the ground. You don't know what long and difficult flights are. I could tell you some stories that would make your hearts stop."

Nicholas said, "We welcome the company because, even for the three of us, it is a long and difficult flight. You must understand that there are times when we cannot slow or stop. If you cannot keep pace, you must fly alone because if we are to survive we must continue."

Henry and Anthony nodded; they understood and agreed.

Henry told Andy and Leroy, but they declined to accompany the others. They were happy with their progress with the two young geese widows. They felt their youth returning and envisioned many adventures here in the town. They had recognized the berry patch, where the hunters used to have their blind. They were keeping an eye on it and had claimed it as their own. The berries were almost ripe.

That night, Henry waited for darkness and then pecked on the Cobbler's door. The Cobbler opened the door and invited Henry into his store. Henry entered and waited for the Cobbler to close the door. The Cobbler led Henry to the back room, where Gilbert still was recovering. The Cobbler removed Henry's artificial foot, and then left to bring some corn, which he spread between Henry and Gilbert. They ate, softly honking, while the Cobbler talked to both of them and evaluated Henry's foot.

The Cobbler studied the artificial foot to see if it had worn evenly or unevenly. He now had a spare one prepared because he never knew when Henry would fly in or fly out. He grabbed it and compared it to the worn one. He continued to talk to Henry and Gilbert as he made some final adjustments. He knew Henry was leaving again. He was very sad because Henry had become like a son to him. He worried about Henry when he was gone, and never knew if or when he would return. He and Henry talked about everything and never argued. Henry made him smile. His nightmares lessened in frequency and intensity. Henry was good for him.

Henry and Gilbert finished the corn and the Cobbler knew it was time. He replaced the new artificial foot on Henry's stump and stood. Henry also stood and honked at Gilbert and turned towards the door. The Cobbler opened it; Henry walked out and turned to honk to the Cobbler. The Cobbler knelt to say good-bye to Henry. Henry rubbed his beak on the Cobbler's outstretched hand, and then he left.

chapter

EIGHTEEN

Early the next morning, Henry, Anthony and the Russians bid Andy, Leroy, and Gilbert goodbye and took to the sky.

Nicholas took the lead because he knew where they were going. They formed a straight line formation. After Nicholas came Dmitry, then Natasha and finally Henry. Anthony followed in Nicholas's draft. In that position, he flew easier than in any of the other positions.

After a couple of hours it was time to change leadership. Henry moved up to the front and everyone else slipped back one position. After a few hours, Anthony's wing hurt and he had difficulty keeping up with the geese.

Henry knew that Anthony could not stay with the group, and honked for Anthony to land on his back. Anthony had to do it while Henry flew. They could not stop because they had to keep flying. Also, each time they landed, they risked being attacked or shot, because there was no guarantee they would land in a friendly place.

Anthony gently caught Henry and settled easily onto his back and grabbed his feathers. This made flying doubly difficult for Henry because he carried Anthony and acted as lead flyer. No sacrifice was too great for a friend.

They stopped early that first night. Henry was exhausted and the others were also tired. It was clear that Anthony could not keep up with the other geese, and Henry, carrying Anthony, also could not keep pace.

When they settled in for the night, before they slept, Nicholas said, "Tomorrow, we take turns leading and we take turns carrying Anthony. Whoever is in the third position will carry Anthony. This way, after you lead, you rest. Then you carry Anthony and then you rest before you lead again." Everyone agreed.

Travel for the next several days was monotonous and the rotation worked well. The group tired faster and could not make as many miles in a day, but they all shared in carrying Anthony. Nicholas, Dmitry, and Natasha understood that Anthony could not be left behind. Anthony was a special friend; one you could always count on when the chips were down. He was little; but what he lacked in size he made up for in heart.

They moved across the Atlantic Ocean, island hopping. They went to Greenland, Iceland, England and then on to France. They swung southeast to fly along the Mediterranean Sea.

Henry was nervous and uncertain. He had similar feelings the day he left home. He was not sure if he was making this trip to spend more time with Natasha, or if the Great Goose was leading him somewhere. He felt something very strong inside, but he did not know exactly what it was.

They would soon arrive in Tula, Russia. Nicholas, Dmitry, and Natasha were very excited about reaching home. Nicholas proudly said, "Mama and Papa will be happy that I have brought everyone home safely. We have traveled far and seen many things. It will be good to be home and settle down."

Dmitry added, "I am sorry to leave so many good friends behind, but it will be good to be home. I wonder if any of the young lady geese have missed me. I bet they have." Dmitry was always optimistic.

Natasha only smiled. It was obvious that she was excited about being home again, but she also was sad at leaving Henry. She liked Henry. He was always a gentleman who could be trusted. Besides her father and brothers, there were not many geese like that.

Anthony felt sad because he had slowed the minigaggle. He was embarrassed and felt useless. He knew that without his friends he would not be alive today. He could not survive alone many days with his aching wing. He wanted to be back in Nebraska, where he could be with all his geese friends. They always took care of each other. Anthony felt that when he protected Henry, he had value, but he felt like an incomplete pigeon when Henry had to carry him on his back. When the other geese had to carry him; he felt completely useless. He knew that Henry did it happily and out of friendship. That made his burden easier to carry.

Henry was very quiet that night. The next morning, as they prepared to start on their last day's flight to reach home, Henry said, "I am sorry, but I can go no farther with you. I have to go south. I will take Anthony because he is my friend, and we take care of each other; however, I must ask a favor from each of you. I need you to come with me. I have never felt such a strong pull. I do not know what it means, but I feel it is urgent and important. I need you"

Anthony paced the ground. He could already smell the excitement and was ready to go. Now he could help Henry. He could repay Henry for his friendship and for carrying him so far. He was ready for Henry to jump into the sky and lead the way.

There was an uncomfortable silence among Nicholas, Dmitry, and Natasha. They silently looked at each other. Henry continued, "I understand if you choose to go home. I will not blame you for not joining us. Nicholas, you have your promise to your Mama and Papa and you are very close to keeping it."

Natasha was the first to nod at Nicholas. Dmitry quickly followed. Nicholas faced Henry and said, "We will follow you wherever you take us. Both of you are brothers to us. You are now part of my promise. I must see all of you safely home."

Henry nodded respectfully at the group and prepared for the trip. Anthony climbed on Henry's back, but

Nicholas said, "No, if Henry is leading, then I will take the third position. Anthony, my brother, jump on my back."

Each of the five felt a strong bond and a strong friendship as they departed. They were nervous since they did not know what to expect. Henry was following the tug on the invisible line. Natasha followed Henry. Nicholas, Dmitry, and Anthony followed Henry and hoped for an experience that they could retell many times in the evenings as they became old. They could already see the younger birds looking at them with respect and awe. They took to flight.

They were not aware that Henry led them south across Turkey and into Syria and then on to Iraq.

An American Marine patrol was checking for insurgent movement west of Baghdad and Fallujah. The patrol consisted of three Hummers and twelve Marines. As they maneuvered about the region, one Hummer stalled. They checked it but could not find the problem. The electronics were not working and they could not restart the engine. The Marine in charge decided to load everyone into the two remaining Hummers and return to base.

The next morning three Marines were sent to retrieve the vehicle. They were to take a tow rope and tow the vehicle to another base nearby, where vehicles were repaired. Sergeant Beck was in charge of the squad. They hoped the operation would be easy since their time in Iraq was almost complete. They should be at the other base by mid-afternoon. They would wait until it was repaired and return to their home base the following day. They were always short of Hummers.

They took a normal amount of gasoline, ammunition, and water. Sergeant Beck drove. A Lance Corporal, known as Ranger Rick, sat in front and another Marine, known as Boozer, sat behind. They had coordinates to follow and within ninety minutes they saw the abandoned Hummer.

As they jumped from their Hummer to secure the tow rope, shots were fired in their direction. They dove behind the vehicles. They tried to see from where the shots came. They spotted two and then three different positions, each only showed one man. Sergeant Beck ordered his men to watch for more insurgents as he tried to reach the lead Hummer to radio for help. Before he could reach the radio, a bullet pierced the gas tank and the Hummer exploded. They now had no communication and no way out. The insurgents had spotted the Hummer and waited, knowing that Marines would try to recover the vehicle.

Sergeant Beck said softly, "OK guys, shoot sparingly. We don't know how long we'll be here, and we don't have ammunition or water for a prolonged engagement with these guys."

Ranger Rick whispered, "I see two more. Do you see the one at about ten o'clock and the second at noon? Do you see the third at about two o'clock? The fourth is behind the first and second man. The fifth is behind the second and third man."

Boozer said, "Yeah, I see them. I wonder how heavily armed they are?"

Sergeant Beck said, "I don't think they have mortars or they would have used them by now. They may have grenades, but they're too far to throw them. They can use their weapons, so we have to be careful. They're too far to represent any threat. They may try to come closer to use their grenades, or they may radio for help, so be alert."

Ranger Rick said, "Should one of us try to flank them tonight? We might be able to have a better shot from the side?"

Sergeant Beck answered, "Perhaps. Right now, we just have to make sure that they don't come any closer."

When the mini-gaggle heard the shots, they quickly landed to evaluate the situation. Henry said, "I think we've found our mission."

Nicholas asked, "Who are the good guys and who are the bad guys?"

Henry said, "I don't know. Does there have to be good guys and bad guys? I think we are supposed to help the humans behind the vehicle."

Dmitry asked, "How do you know that? Are you sure?"

Henry said confidently, "I am certain they are the ones we are supposed to help."

Anthony asked Henry, "How can the Great Goose determine which group should be helped and which group should be hurt?"

Henry was quiet for a moment before responding, "If we help the ones hiding behind the sand, they will kill the others, even if they do not need to kill them. If we help the ones behind the vehicle, they will only hurt the others if they have to hurt them. I feel that is what will happen. It is not a situation where one group is right and the other is wrong. We may hurt some men, but they need not die."

Nicholas asked Henry, "What do we do?"

"Anthony and I must find help for the humans. You three should stay here and protect the humans behind the vehicle as you would protect your own nest. Anthony and I will bring help. You must be careful because no human will know if you are helping or not. Any one of them may try to shot you."

Anthony climbed on Henry's back, and Henry jumped into the sky, went around the humans and then turned south.

Nicholas turned to Natasha and ordered, "You stay here. Dmitry and I will take a look around and we'll be back in a few minutes." They took flight.

They flew around the back of the insurgents and then swung around the back of the humans behind the vehicle.

Boozer was the first to see them. "Hey, you guys, look at that! What the heck is that? I've never seen birds that big. The only thing I've seen in this sand pile is those little bitty birds. Look at those birds! How much do you think they weigh? Do you think they would be good eating?"

Ranger Rick said, "Yep, those are big birds, but I have no idea what they are. They seem to be circling us. I wish I had my shotgun. They're not buzzards, are they?"

Sergeant Beck said, "No one shoots at any bird no matter how big it is. We have a bigger problem here. Let's stay focused."

Nicholas and Dmitry returned to where Natasha was waiting. Nicholas said "Dmitry and I will continue to circle the humans behind the sand. If any one of them stands or walks, we will knock him down. Natasha, you wait for us.

Whatever happens, you do not leave the ground." With that, Nicholas and Dmitry returned to the sky.

After a while insurgent number four started walking to insurgent number one. The Marines had not yet fired, and he did not seem worried. He was not aware that Nicholas and Dmitry had noticed his movements and the geese quickly swung around, crossed wings, and rapidly made their silent approach. Insurgent number four never knew what hit him. He flipped and his rifle flew from his hands. Insurgent number one jumped when Nicholas and Dmitry silently flew over him from behind. Only when he turned around did he see his colleague lying on the ground.

Boozer yelled, "Did you guys just see that? Those two birds just clipped one of the insurgents. Look at him. He doesn't know what hit him."

Sergeant Beck said, "I saw it, but I don't believe it. Stay alert guys. They may be planning something."

As Henry left the others, he told Anthony, "I don't know where we should go to find help, Anthony. You must focus. You're a homing pigeon. Home-in on where we need to go."

Anthony was very annoyed at the reminder of his weakness and said, "Henry, Homing Pigeons have to have a home before they can find it. The place we are trying to find is not my home. I can't just take us there. How can I take you to a place where I have never been?"

Henry said, "Anthony, you must focus and imagine where the place is so we can find help. It's urgent. Don't you know any tricks? We need a miracle."

Anthony said, "As long as you're talking to me how can I concentrate?"

He remembered his mother telling him that if he needed help to call on her. She would appear and lead him where he needed to go. Anthony began to focus on his mother. Minutes passed while Henry flew farther and farther. Suddenly, he looked ahead and saw his mother far ahead of them. She moved to the left so Anthony told Henry to turn left. For the next hour Henry followed Anthony's directions, and Anthony followed his mother.

In the distance, Henry saw many vehicles and tents and he went to them. Anthony's mother suddenly disappeared. As Henry approached the tents and humans, he did not know where to go. What if one of them shot at them? He leveled off and escaped notice. Suddenly, he appeared on the edge of the encampment and several Marines saw him at once. He landed and Anthony jumped to the ground. A large group of Marines stared at them without saying a word. Their mouths were open and they were silent. This is not a common site for Marines to see.

One alert Marine brought Henry and Anthony's arrival to the attention of a Captain. They both returned and stared at Henry and Anthony. Henry honked, took a few steps and stopped. He did not know with whom he should talk or whom he should approach. He repeated his honks. Anthony kept his distance but was very alert. If any one of these humans tried to hurt Henry, he would find himself without any eyes.

The Marines continued to stare. One Marine Lance Corporal, known as Mud Flap, gathered his wits and said, "Isn't that a pigeon and a goose?"

Another Marine, known as Tootsie Roll, added, "And isn't the goose wearing a shoe?"

Still another Marine, known as Gravy, asked, "Didn't the pigeon fly in on the goose's back?"

The Captain felt he needed to say something, so he said, "Yep! Yep! Yep!"

Marine, Bevis said, "I grew up around geese on the Platte River. There're probably no other geese within a thousand miles of here. There're probably no Canada geese within two or three thousand miles from here. Something is strange here."

Mud Flap mocked, "No kidding, Sherlock."

Henry was anxious. He honked for Anthony to jump on, which he did. The Marine's mouths collectively dropped open again. Henry began walking away. He took a few steps, stopped and looked to see if anyone followed. They were not. They just stared at Henry and Anthony.

Henry decided on a new approach. He told Anthony to hang on, and he jumped into the sky. He flew north towards the stranded Marines, but then he returned and landed. He took a few steps and watched to see if anyone followed. They did not. Henry became frustrated and asked the Great Goose for help.

Gravy said, "Hey, any of you guys ever watch "Lassie' on TV? When Lassie wanted people to follow her, she would behave about the same way. Is it possible that the goose wants us to follow it?"

The Captain, tired of this situation that made no sense to him, said, "Bring a Hummer around. Lance Corporal Bevis, grab two more men and some extra ammo and we'll follow these birds. Anybody know what the chances are they're working for the insurgents, leading us into a trap?"

Mud Flat yelled, "Tootsie Roll, Gravy, fall in."

The Hummer appeared, everyone climbed in, and the Captain yelled, "I don't want to hear any jokes about this if it turns out to be nothing. Anyone that makes any smart comments will have extra duty until the day he returns to the States." The Captain gave the command and they started.

Henry and Anthony already were circling while waiting for the Marines. When they saw the vehicle following them, Henry asked Anthony to find the stranded Marines. Anthony cleared his mind and focused again on his mother. Within a minute or so she appeared about fifty yards in front of him. Anthony could barely see her. Anthony guided Henry and they headed north as fast as Henry could fly. They flew low so that the Marines could see them.

chapter

NINTEEN

After Nicholas and Dmitry clipped the standing insurgent, they stayed in their foxholes. They occasionally shot at the Marines, but the objective was to keep the Marines in their position. The insurgents were too far from the Marines to hit them.

Sergeant Beck expected more insurgents to arrive soon. He considered slipping away at night and walking back to camp, but it would be easy to become disoriented in the desert and never reach camp. He also felt that home base might realize that they had not completed their mission and; therefore, a rescue mission might soon arrive. If this happened, they would need to stay with the stranded Hummer to facilitate their rescue.

Boozer looked up and said, "Do you see that dust on the horizon? Is that a dust storm or are more vehicles coming this way?"

Sergeant Beck said, "Gentlemen, check your weapons and your ammunition. I think our friends are receiving reinforcements. They may have brought weapons that can hit us. Let's move back about fifty yards and dig in. They'll aim at the Hummer first. If they advance, we will need to redeploy farther to the rear. Two of us will cover the third as he moves. We'll do this in ten yard increments. Are there any questions? Let's go."

Nicholas, Dmitry and Natasha also saw the dust. Nicholas said, "Both of you stay here. I'm going to make a wide circle around them to see what they have."

Two pickups arrived. They had jet-propelled grenade launchers (JPGs) and mortars. There were ten more fighters. They stopped near the closest manned position; the fighters piled out and grabbed their equipment. They ran to the leader of the group, who explained the situation as he pointed towards the stalled Hummer. He then motioned instructions to each fighter to let them know where they were supposed to position themselves.

The men spread out, while one man fired a JPG. The Hummer lifted from the ground and was enveloped in flames. They waited for retaliation. None came. Sergeant Beck thought the insurgents did not know exactly where they were. This made it difficult for them to aim anything accurately at them. As the fire reached the tires, the smoke turned black and formed a column reaching into the sky.

Three insurgents confidently stood upright near their two vehicles. They talked and pointed. They did not notice the three huge birds circling behind them. Nicholas, Dmitry, and Natasha prepared for their first strike. There were too many humans involved, and they could no longer double-team them. Each had to strike one human. They identified their targets and silently sped towards them. They each clipped their intended target at the base of his neck. The insurgents fell like rag dolls. The other insurgents were surprised to see these large and unknown birds. One insurgent fired crazily with his weapon at the geese, but they were never in danger, as they entered Henry's cork-screw formation and rapidly gained altitude. Another insurgent yelled at the shooter and he quickly stopped shooting. No one noticed the three men behind them slowly sitting up and rubbing the backs of their necks.

Henry and Anthony both saw the dark smoke in the distance and Henry tried to fly faster. The Captain also saw it and grabbed the radio to call his base. He ordered more Marines and Hummers immediately. They proceeded as fast as possible and would engage the enemy on sight.

Two insurgents looked back and saw that their leaders were hurt. They ran to help. Nicholas and Dmitry swung around, and as the insurgents reached down to help their friends, they were clipped from behind. They spun around and one rifle discharged, hitting another insurgent in the shoulder. Five insurgents were on the ground, confused, with neck injuries.

The insurgents decided they would have five men charge the Marines, although they were not sure where the Marines were. Since the mortar attack, they had not seen any Marines. The remaining insurgents would cover their charge. They reasoned that when the Marines revealed their positions, the insurgents could use mortars and JPGs to end the fight.

The five insurgents started running, and then they dropped. They kept repeating this procedure, advancing ten to fifteen yards each run. Nicholas, Dmitry, and Natasha circled and timed their flight.

The Marines watched the developments and were surprised by their unexpected allies, but they also prepared for the rush attack. They had their targets in sight, when three of their targets flipped over and lay still on the ground. The Marines smiled, looked at each other, and held their fire.

As the goose squad swung around, the insurgents began firing at the geese, as they now recognized the geese as enemies. The geese cork-screwed through the sky and were very hard to track. Three insurgents forgot that the Marines were behind them and they stood to shoot at the geese squad. Henry and Anthony arrived. Anthony jumped off Henry's back, allowing Henry to fly faster. Henry flew down the insurgent line honking and flying in his cork-screw formation. The insurgents forgot about Nicholas, Dmitry and Natasha and began shooting wildly at Henry.

Anthony, following Henry, picked the closest insurgent and went for his face. He tried to grab his eyeballs with his feet to squeeze them, but he only found his nose. He bit his nose with all his might. The man screamed and ran wildly, trying to pull Anthony from his face. Every time he tried to pull Anthony off, he increased his own pain because Anthony did not release his nose. Finally, the insurgent used his fist and hit Anthony on his back. Anthony felt horrible pain and had to release his grip. He fell to the sand and lay still. He looked up at the man he had attacked, and even in intense pain, smiled broadly. Anthony was pleased with his results, but he hurt.

The insurgent grabbed his face and screamed. Another insurgent came over and pointed his weapon at Anthony. Before he could pull the trigger, the shooter, the screaming insurgent, and another were silently clipped from behind as Nicholas, Dmitry, and Natasha swung around again. The three insurgents lay on the ground, stunned and confused.

The Captain arrived at the battle, but was not noticed except by the other Marines. They stood and walked over to the Captain. Sergeant Beck said, "Do you think they need our help? I've counted eleven insurgents down, and we haven't fired a shot."

As they watched, Henry did another corkscrew maneuver over the remaining insurgents to keep their attention away from Nicholas, Dmitry, and Natasha. An insurgent stood and threw a hand grenade in front of Henry. The blast blew Henry several yards. He hit the ground hard and did not move. He tried to feel each part of his body to assess the damage. His left wing hurt and he could not move it. The insurgent, who threw the grenade, was double-teamed by Nicholas and Dmitry. He also did not move once he hit the ground.

Sergeant Beck said, "Captain, I think we should make our presence known. The geese have done what they can. It's time for us to do our part now."

The Captain, agreeing, barked, "Spread out and prepare to take prisoners."

The Marines spread out and the Captain fired a few rounds near the remaining insurgents. They spun around and saw the seven Marines and their firepower. They dropped their weapons and held their hands high. While some Marines guarded, the others searched their prisoners, removing weapons and securing their hands behind their backs. They radioed for transport for fifteen prisoners.

Nicholas and Natasha flew to Henry while Dmitry flew to Anthony.

Henry lay on his back, and his feet moved slowly. His left wing was bleeding as was his chest, and he was not able to turn over. Nicholas and Natasha gently went to his side and used their beaks to help Henry roll over. His left wing looked mangled. Nicholas and Natasha honked softly to encourage Henry, but they knew he was hurt seriously.

Dmitry found Anthony also lying on the ground, right side up. Anthony's wing looked very bad. Anthony said nothing because the pain was great. Dmitry stayed with Anthony and tried to comfort him, honking softly and using his beak to rub on Anthony's short neck. Anthony understood the gesture and cooed back at him in appreciation.

Sergeant Beck was the first to remember the geese. He turned and saw the two groups of geese. He slowly approached Anthony and Dmitry. Sergeant Beck looked at Anthony; Anthony returned the look. Dmitry took a few steps back, but also looked at Sergeant Beck. Sergeant Beck was certain that he saw pleading in their eyes.

Avoiding sudden moves, Sergeant Beck went to the other group. He saw Henry with his bloody wing, and his feet moving uselessly. He quickly returned to the Captain.

"Captain," he said, "we need a Doc for these birds. They're hurt bad."

The Captain did not answer immediately. He wondered how other people would view this request. He also thought about what the geese had done for them. He never would have believed it if he had not seen it for himself. Loyalty in the Marines goes deep.

He grabbed the radio and asked, "Base Camp? This is Captain Waters. I need a Medivac. We have two men down."

The Captain looked at Sergeant Beck and said nothing. It was obvious that he was worried how this request might end.

Henry looked at Natasha and Nicholas and said, "Thank you for your help, my friends. We couldn't have done it without you. Now, you must continue your trip home. Anthony and I cannot accompany you. We do not know what will happen to us. We depend completely on the humans. If they leave us here, we will die, but you must go home or you will die also."

Nicholas was silent. Natasha cried. After a few moments, Nicholas said, "You are right, Henry, my brother. We will leave and return home, but we will not forget you. It is possible that one day we will see each other again. We trust that your Great Goose will not abandon you now and that we will see each other again."

Both Nicholas and Natasha rubbed their beaks on Henry's neck. Henry honked acknowledgment.

Nicholas flew to Dmitry. Natasha did not move. Nicholas informed Dmitry of their decision. Nicholas said goodbye to his little fiery friend, Anthony, and Dmitry flew to Henry to say goodbye. Nicholas and Dmitry jumped into the sky and began to circle. Natasha did not move. Nicholas honked, and Natasha reluctantly joined them. They quickly disappeared into the horizon.

Sergeant Beck slowly approached Anthony and started talking to him. "Easy fellow. I'm not going to hurt you. I'm going to pick you up and put you next to your crazy friend. Easy now."

Anthony was not happy to see a human approaching him, but there was nothing he could do. The voice did not sound like he was going to hurt him. Sergeant Beck slowly reached down and cupped Anthony in his hands very carefully. He took him to Henry and placed him gently beside him. When they saw each other, Anthony cooed and Henry honked. By this time, Ranger Rick and Boozer slowly and respectfully approached the two birds. Ranger Rick said, "Did you guys see the goose's white foot? What's that?"

Boozer said, "That doesn't look like his real foot. Do you suppose he had that shot off someplace else?"

Sergeant Beck asked, "What's that on his foot?"

Boozer answered, "Blood. Isn't that blood?"

Sergeant Beck said, "No, not the blood. The other stuff."

He took his finger and carefully tried to uncover it.

He said, "They're numbers. Doesn't that look like a telephone number? Boozer, write that number down."

Boozer said, "It's probably the CIA's number. Maybe we'll receive a reward for recovering these birds."

Sergeant Beck said, "That's it Boozer. You stay in the Marine Corps and you'll go home a general. You've the brain power and the imagination for it."

The helicopter arrived and scared the stuffing out of both Henry and Anthony, but Sergeant Beck knelt beside them and talked softly to them. That helped to calm them.

The corpsman and his assistant jumped from the helicopter. The corpsman asked, "Hey Cap, where're the wounded?"

The Captain pointed to Sergeant Beck, kneeling and said, "It looks like they may have broken wings."

The technicians stopped and turned towards the Captain. The corpsman asked, "Did you say 'broken wings'? Are you pulling our legs?"

The Captain replied, without hiding his annoyance, "Yes, I said 'broken wings.' No, I am not pulling your leg. Now, if those two don't make a full recovery, I will come after you. Treat the patients, now." The corpsman jumped into action.

The corpsman approached his patients and said, "Holy moly, it's a pigeon and a goose!"

He started to examine them carefully for wounds other than the obvious broken wings. He told his partner, "We need to deaden the pain because those breaks are bad. They must hurt like a son of a gun." He paused and then asked, "How much should we give each one? We could easily kill them if we give them too much."

His partner said, "The normal dosage is for a one hundred, seventy-five pound man. The pigeon must weigh about one pound and the goose must weigh ten to fifteen pounds."

The chief technician said, "Let's be conservative because if we give too much, they could die. If we give too little, they'll simply feel pain."

They did the calculations, prepared the injections, and gave them. They asked for Sergeant Beck and Ranger Rick to each hold a bird. Boozer said, "They helped save my behind, too. You're not leaving me out of this."

The corpsman said, "Fine, you can hold this," and he handed him his medical bag.

They boarded the helicopter and lifted off. The corpsman said, "We may have given the pigeon too much pain killer."

The assistant asked, "Why do you say that?"

The corpsman said, "Have you ever seen a pigeon smile like that? He doesn't appear to be feeling any pain."

When they landed, the helicopter was met by the base's commanding officer. When he saw Henry and Anthony cradled in the arms of two Marines and no other wounded, he yelled, "Captain Waters, what is the meaning of this? Where did you find these two birds?"

Captain Waters took off his helmet and ran his other hand through his hair. He knew this question was coming and he had rehearsed the answer.

"General," said Captain Waters, "you are not going to believe this." He proceeded to tell the story.

He was right. The General asked, "And the other Marines can confirm this idiotic story?"

"Yes, sir," replied the Captain.

Henry and Anthony were taken to the Field Hospital, where the base maintained two doctors. They had only minimal equipment since all serious medical work was done at a military hospital in Germany. They did have an x-ray machine. The doctors were surprised at their two new patients, but they were always quick to respond to an emergency. They would worry later about how normal this emergency was.

Henry was x-rayed and examined. His body was bruised from the grenade, but his left wing was broken. Anthony was fortunate that his assailant hit where he did or his back might have been broken. The same wing that he had broken fighting the coyote was broken again.

The doctor said, "This wasn't the first time the pigeon has broken this wing. I don't know how he has been flying because his wing did not heal properly the first time."

One doctor had benefited from some time in a children's orthopedic ward at a hospital. He checked the x-rays and saw that he could set the wings. With appropriate pins and screws, they could fly again. He took dimensions for pins and screws for both Henry and Anthony. They did not have any of the right size in stock, so he contacted another hospital and they sent them immediately.

The doctors set both wings as best as they could. They improvised splints to immobilize their wings and made them more comfortable until the pins and screws arrived. Sergeant Beck was placed in charge of meeting their needs until their wings could be surgically repaired.

He called for Ranger Rick and Boozer to help him take the patients to their tent. They prepared an area between the cots of Sergeant Beck and Ranger Rick. They found some plastic four feet square and placed it between their cots. They put some water there. They sent Boozer for some food. He returned with bread, crackers without salt, and fruit. All three Marines tried to feed Henry and Anthony, who gratefully accepted food from one Marine and then another.

Sergeant Beck asked Ranger Rick for the telephone number. Sergeant Beck said, "I'm going to buy a phone card and call this number. I have to know what it is."

One hour later, Sergeant Beck was at the phone bank and the number he dialed was ringing. It rang several times before a voice answered, "Yes."

Sergeant Beck said, "Please do not hang up until I can ask a few questions. This is a serious call. We found your phone number on a white shoe worn by a Canada goose." Sergeant Beck expected the voice to hang up the phone.

The voice quickly responded, "Yes. That would be Henry. Do you have him? Is he alright? Where are you?"

Sergeant Beck breathed deeply not believing his ears. He answered, "This is Sergeant Beck. I am a Marine in Iraq. We have Henry and a pigeon. Both have been wounded in action. They are fine. They each have a broken wing which is being treated."

The Cobbler gasped, "Wounded in action? Iraq? Are you serious?"

Sergeant Beck explained briefly what had happened and the Cobbler became very nervous. He reacted the same way that any parent would react when they receive a phone call from the military informing them that their child has been wounded in action. The Cobbler became very emotional and had to apply great restraint or he would have cried and been unable to talk.

The Cobbler asked, "Were Henry and Anthony alone in the attack or were other birds there?"

Sergeant Beck replied, "There were three very large birds. We have no idea what they were, but they were not wounded and left following the engagement."

The Cobbler said, "Yes. Those are Tula geese. They are from the Ukrainian and Russian regions. They may have gone home."

Sergeant Beck said, "I should be returned to the U.S. soon, as my time in Iraq will be over in a couple of weeks. If you tell me where you live, I will personally deliver Henry and Anthony to you."

The Cobbler gave his address. Sergeant Beck gave the Cobbler his family's phone number in Illinois and they said goodbye.

Within a couple of days the pins and screws arrived, and Henry and Anthony had their surgery. The doctors thought that it was successful, but their wings would have to remain immobilized for a long time.

Sergeant Beck visited the Captain and asked, "Captain, when our platoon returns in a few days, may I take the goose and the pigeon?"

The Captain wished that the two birds would disappear because they did not fit into any of the military's many regulations. He was trapped. He could not abandon anyone who fought with him, no matter what the consequences. He said, "I will obtain the necessary papers for them to accompany you on your ship to the States; however, you and your accomplices must take full responsibility for their care on board the ship."

He thought a moment and then continued, "What are you going to do with them when you arrive in the States?"

Sergeant Beck said, "I found the man who made Henry's prosthetic foot. He lives in Nebraska. I will deliver Henry and Anthony to him. It seems they have a long-standing relationship."

The Captain asked, "They have names? Henry and Anthony?"

Sergeant Beck said, "Yes. And Sir, the other birds were Tula geese. They were Russian."

The Captain immediately stopped what he was doing. He looked at Sergeant Beck and begged, "Please tell no one else that the Russians helped us in combat. That is all that I need. We could easily have an international situation. My career could be destroyed if that became known."

The highest authority was informed about the situation. Within hours, a gag order was in place. No one could talk about what happened. No one could mention geese, especially Russian geese. The Captain said, "Darn it, anyway. This is becoming too complicated."

chapter

TWENTY

Within a few days, the 7th Engineering Company C 1st and 2nd Platoons from Peoria, Illinois were on board ship, sailing towards America. Sergeant Beck, Ranger Rick and Boozer bunked next to each other. They cleared a small area and placed boards around it allowing Henry and Anthony to come and go as they pleased while keeping the Marines from stepping inside Henry and Anthony's safe area.

No Marine pestered Henry and Anthony; they were treated with respect. They were treated as Marines returning from combat duty. When Henry and Anthony walked by, the Marines stopped their small talk and joking and all eyes were on the two heroes. It was as if a general had appeared, only they did not have to come to attention and salute. Their respectful silence was their salute. They did not know what else to do since they did not know how to talk to a goose and a pigeon.

Each day the Marines were allocated a specified amount of time on deck for fresh air and exercise. At first, Sergeant Beck, Ranger Rick and Boozer went on deck alone, after ensuring that Henry and Anthony were safe in their box. After a couple of days they felt guilty and tried to think of a way to take them on deck also. The problem was that they might try to fly or become frightened and fall overboard. If they did that, they would be doomed without the use of their wings.

Sergeant Beck, a graduate of Southern Illinois University at Edwardsville (SIUE) in Mechanical Engineering, was the first to propose a plan. He suggested that they place Henry in a harness that prevented his wings from unfolding, yet would allow him to hang freely from a frame that they would carry. They could attach Anthony in a similar fashion, but above Henry, like when Henry carried Antony on his back. The plan was immediately approved and work started.

They had to find straps for the harnesses. How and where they found the straps cannot be revealed, but some officers soon found their belts had disappeared. Other Marines heard of the plan and joined in the project. There were two Marines who had worked with leather in high school, and this would be similar. Sergeant Beck sketched the harnesses and the volunteers started cutting and fastening the pieces.

Ranger Rick designed the frame, which, when Henry and Anthony were attached, would be carried by two Marines. A great discussion ensued because so many Marines wanted to carry the heroes. The frame had to be redesigned for four Marines to carry them; two in front and two behind. A sign-up sheet was prepared so any four Marines, who wanted to share their on-deck exercise time with Henry and Anthony, could do so. The sheet was filled in minutes.

The strap workers tried the harnesses on Henry and Anthony and then made some adjustments. The harnesses were again attached to Henry and Anthony and then to the frame. Four Marines lifted the frames slowly to remove the slack, and Henry and Anthony felt themselves becoming airborne. They both smiled and looked around gratefully at their friends. Marines never leave their wounded behind, and they always take care of them. The Marines were pleased.

The first group to take the Henry and Anthony on deck consisted of Sergeant Beck, Ranger Rick, Boozer and Tootsie Roll. Once on deck they connected all the fasteners and started around the ship while marching in-step. Tootsie Roll became so excited with the honor that he started calling cadence: one, two, three, four, one, two, three, four. Each of the Marines sharpened his step and Henry and Anthony felt the sea breeze on their faces. They were happy and their smiles were easily seen. Henry stretched his neck out and leaned forward as he would if he were flying. It was obvious to everyone that Henry wanted to fly again. Anthony; however, enjoyed it, but his eyes also demonstrated reluctance.

A passing sailor saw the parade and asked, "Is that for the Captain's lunch? I know he loves goose, but the pigeon I don't think he'll like. Him, you can throw overboard, unless you guys want him." Ranger Rick, Boozer and Tootsie Roll started to set the frame down to fight the wise-cracking sailor.

Sergeant Beck prevented the fight when he said, "Guys! Guys! If you start a fight you'll end up in the brig and then you can't escort Henry and Anthony." Boozer said, "That sailor get away with that disrespect. We have to teach him a lesson." Beck said, "That sailor has no idea what Henry and Anthony did for us, and suggest you keep it that way. Do you want to be the one to explain to him what these guys did? I don't think they would believe you. Some things are better left alone." That refocused the group on taking care of business.

When the first group's time ended, four more Marines met them at the door to relieve the first group. Henry and Anthony spent the entire day marching around the ship's deck. Some Marines developed their own routines with Henry and Anthony. Each group created its own marching songs and routines. One group would march as usual with their arms hanging down, then; they would bend their elbow up so that the frame would be shoulder level, and finally; they would fully extend their arms upward. Henry and Anthony seemed to love the notoriety and the variety, but most of all they loved the fresh air and feeling of flight.

Sergeant Beck, watched Henry's and Anthony's reaction to being carried around the deck, and had an idea. He had been a member the SIUE team that built a robot and entered it into a national contest. Their robot won the contest. Why could they not build a giant wing, or a huge kite, that could fly with Henry and Anthony suspended? They still would not be flying with their own wings, but they would be flying.

Sergeant Beck gained access to a computer and emailed his professor at SIUE about the situation. He gave the approximate weights of Henry and Anthony and specified that Anthony would be suspended above Henry's back and both would fly from the same wing.

The professor gathered the winning robotics team and presented them with the problem. They divided tasks and started research. The professor also had a friend who worked in the aeronautic industry and contacted him.

Within a couple of days, Sergeant Beck received an email, which had plans they could use to build a wing. A copy was printed and he returned to present it to the Marine task force. The first problem was the supports. They liberated some aluminum tubing and gained access to the metal shop on board. They traded Iraq souvenirs for welding.

The fabric was a problem until one Marine remembered parachutes. With many people working, it did not take long to produce the first prototype. They took the main pieces of the frame on deck and connected them. One Marine went to the mess hall and returned with a fifteen-pound bag of flour. He took it on deck and it was fastened in a harness. Another Marine went to the prow of the deck and secured the line. Two Marines balanced the wing until it caught some air and lifted gently, easily lifting the load. They could control the height of the wing by the length of the rope. They would have to be careful not to allow their heroes to fly too high.

The Marine returned the flour to the mess hall. The cook looked at him suspiciously, and opened the sack, felt and smelled the flour before he grunted and accepted it.

Sergeant Beck and Ranger Rick went to fetch Henry and Anthony. About thirty Marines watched. They carefully attached Henry and then Anthony. They double-checked each harness and each part of the kite. The Marine in front tied the kite to the ship after carefully measuring the distance. The two Marines at each wing tip carefully tipped the wing so that it would catch the breeze. They felt its pull and then Henry and Anthony were up. They smiled so much that they swallowed their ears. Henry honked excitedly and Anthony cooed. The Marines cheered. It was a very joyous occasion.

Each day Henry and Anthony spent hours flying above the deck. The Marines posted guards continually to ensure that they did not leave the ship's airspace, and they protected Henry and Anthony from the sailors who wanted Henry for other reasons.

On their last day on board the ship, a group of Marines requested a formation. They asked that Sergeant Beck, Ranger Rick, Boozer and Henry and Anthony be present. Sergeant Beck thought it sounded mysterious but the meeting was arranged. Sergeant Beck and the others did not know that the meeting had been cleared earlier by the Captain, who had witnessed Henry's and Anthony's bravery.

When Sergeant Beck and his group appeared on deck, they were shocked to see the two platoons of combat engineers from Peoria, Illinois on deck, in dress uniforms. The Marine band was also present and started playing the Marine's Hymn when the three rescued Marines and Henry and Anthony appeared. Henry and Anthony had long since become accustomed to the ship's noises and were only mildly frightened.

Gravy, who had accompanied the Captain in rescuing the stranded Marines, and who had witnessed the heroics of Henry and Anthony, stepped forward in top Marine form. When he stopped in front of the group, he shouted, "Permission to speak Sergeant!"

Sergeant Beck said, "Granted," and wondered what would follow.

"Sergeant, the other Marines and I think that Henry and Anthony deserve more recognition for what they did. We have been informed that we cannot discuss what we saw that day with anyone outside our platoon. We have urged that they be recommended for Purple Hearts, but our request has been denied. We discussed this and decided that we could do something on our own. Several Marines have donated pieces of gold jewelry, which we melted. We made a mold of the Purple Heart medal and we have made two golden Purple Hearts. We wish to award Henry and Anthony with these. Sergeant, will you see that whoever cares for them receives these medals?"

Sergeant Beck, Ranger Rick and Boozer were moved by this gesture. They only wished that they could make Henry and Anthony understand the honor they had just received.

The ship arrived and the Marines were sent to Camp Lejeune for a few weeks of transitional time. It is difficult to transition from a war zone in a foreign country to peace in your own country. Men experiencing combat need time to prepare themselves to return to their civilian lives. The two weeks in Camp Lejeune gave them a chance to transition to civilian life.

When Sergeant Beck was given his official discharge from the Marines, he made plans to return Henry and Anthony to the Cobbler. Ranger Rick and Boozer insisted that they make the trip as a team. They did not consider their mission complete until Henry and Anthony had been safely returned to the Cobbler in Nebraska.

They were flown to Peoria, Illinois where they rented an SUV and went to Nebraska. Henry and Anthony were placed in cages to maintain the vehicle's cleanliness.

They called the Cobbler and told him that they would arrive by late afternoon. They maintained their schedule and arrived by 4:00 p.m. They found his shop and walked in the front door carrying Henry and Anthony. The Cobbler, seeing the Marines with Henry and Antony, froze momentarily. It was apparent that he was becoming emotional and was struggling to control it. After a few seconds, he stepped forward and shook their hands and knelt to inspect Henry and Anthony. When he found them in good condition, beyond their broken wings, he stood and thanked the Marines again. He offered coffee, which he joyously prepared. He looked around to find three chairs and asked them to sit. As he positioned the coffee pot on the table before loading it with coffee, he looked back at the Marines and Henry. Sergeant Beck recognized the Cobbler's need to do and say everything at once and his inability to do or say anything. Sergeant Beck suggested that the Cobbler relax and concentrate on the coffee and his squad would tell every detail of the story of Henry and Anthony's heroism.

After two cups of coffee, they finished the story and Sergeant Beck presented him with the two golden Purple Hearts. He explained the circumstances and origin of these medals and gave the Cobbler the details of how they were wounded; even though they were sworn to secrecy. He told the Cobbler that he was giving him this information because he was responsible for Henry and Anthony and deserved to know; plus, the Cobbler was a Marine and understood.

The Cobbler was continuously giving Henry and Anthony corn, which they accepted graciously. The four Marines talked late into the night and agreed to meet the next morning. The three Marines spent the night in a motel and then met one last time with the Cobbler and Henry and Anthony. They had to teach the Cobbler how to use the kite to suspend Henry and Anthony.

That night, after the Marines left, the Cobbler took Henry and Anthony to the fountain for a swim. Henry swam happily and Anthony sat on the edge and watched. It was a peaceful fountain in a peaceful town. It was not long before Gilbert arrived. His wing was better now and he was flying normally. Andy and Leroy arrived, accompanied by the two young widows. Andy and Leroy were excited to see Henry and Anthony. They spent almost an hour together honking and cooing. Then the Cobbler took Henry and Anthony inside for the evening and fed them again.

After a restful night, the group met the next morning and took Henry, Anthony, and the kite to the park. The local citizens saw Henry, Anthony, the kite, the Cobbler, and the three Marines in full uniform and they knew that something interesting was going to happen. A crowd developed behind them as they walked to the park.

At the park they put Henry and Anthony into their harnesses and then assembled the wing. The harness and the wing were connected and Ranger Rick and the Cobbler held the wings, while Sergeant Beck uncoiled some of the strong string, which secured the wing. Then Sergeant Beck started running, as did the other two Marines, and very quickly Henry and Anthony rose into the air. Henry honked. Anthony cooed. The spectators clapped, and the Marines smiled. The Cobbler had tears in his eyes, but no one looked at him.

Later, the three Marines said goodbye to the Cobbler, Henry and Anthony, and they left to start their civilian lives.

The Cobbler was seen every day making his trip to the park with Henry and Anthony. The Cobbler now spoke with everyone and always smiled. Young boys and girls fought to gain the honored position of holding the wings. Some days the Cobbler took Henry and Anthony to the Platte River, where he secured their kite to his car. He slowly drove up and down the pastures with Henry and Anthony floating happily.

It was impossible to determine which of the three was the happiest: the Cobbler, Henry or Anthony. They were a team. They were a family. And they were happy.